DEATH
of a
GRIM REAPER

BALI FIELDS

First Edition

An original publication of Clonakilty Publications

ISBN-10: 0989006700
ISBN-13: 9780989006705

For information on upcoming events, please visit
www.deathofagrimreaper.com or follow Bali Fields on Facebook

The author wishes to thank the living and the dead.

For Cynthia,
the brown eyed woman
who filled my world with life

I know what it's like to be dead...

She Said She Said

John Lennon & Paul McCartney

DEATH
of a
GRIM REAPER

1

It was time to reap a soul. Cornelius spirited up the coast of Georgia clutching his scythe and banked left over Savannah, riding a southwesterly sea breeze to Ocilla.

The curtains of the house at 78 Dewberry Road were frayed at the bottom. Sprawling cobwebs glistened on a dust-covered chandelier and mold spores hid under the wallpaper. Termites made tracks on the wood floor as if leaving a trail of breadcrumbs. Cornelius waited as Eleanor came down the hall wearing a housecoat and a pair of worn slippers. He struggled to come up with a way to execute the deed; a death had to appear natural. Cadets had leeway on how to harvest a soul, and originality and simplicity were highly valued. He rechecked The Book of Expiration Dates—Eleanor had four minutes to live.

According to the biographical scroll, ninety two year-old Eleanor Swanson, Ellie around the neighborhood, had a resilient heart and a will to live as strong as a Joshua tree. As a girl, Ellie played with the "negroes" down the road. Easy enough as a child to be unaware of racism, but as an adolescent growing up in the American south during the

1930s, learning the prejudices of the day was practically a rite of passage. Ellie resisted the ignorance and was struck by a policeman with a nightstick on Bloody Sunday during one of the Selma to Montgomery marches of 1965, gaining a lifelong scar over her left eyebrow.

Cornelius put away the scroll. Although unsure how to reap Ellie, he relished the challenge, only yesterday he was a bureaucrat working in the cave of the Replanting Department transmuting vile mortal souls to undesirable lives as aye-ayes, gulper eels, and naked mole rats. Now, promoted to Grim Reaper Cadet, he had the privilege of spiriting up and down the east coast of North America from the Canadian Arctic to the Florida Keys.

The hall was dark so he decided to set up a fall and pushed up the edge of the Turkish carpet. Eleanor teetered, but kept walking. One minute to go. Cornelius spirited to the bathroom and assessed the area. A neighbor had installed grab bars, and elder services provided an elevated toilet seat to ease the ups and downs. It was a long trip back to the Dwelling, so he lapped up Universal Elixir from the dripping faucet, before sprinkling a few droplets on the bare floor.

Ellie made it past the quarter-inch threshold, but slipped on the wet tiles, hit the clawfoot tub and fell to floor, fracturing her hip. Cornelius shuddered at the ugly mash-up of sounds created by splintering bone and the shriek of an elderly woman. When it was safe, he materialized and leaned down to examine the medical alert device lying on the floor—when suddenly Ellie opened her eyes and reached for it. They made eye contact. He panicked and slammed down the scythe.

The house was absolutely silent. It was as if it had died, too. Cornelius drifted to the open window, and looking back, wondered how long it would take for someone to find Ellie and give her a proper burial.

He rode the prevailing winds over the Atlantic Ocean toward the Dwelling. The cadet dorm was situated on a spit of rock sticking up out of the ocean, part of the Svalbard archipelago of Norway. Perpetually covered with snow and ice, the Dwelling lacked value to mortals, but it gave cadets a place to rest. There were five chambers—upright cylindrical sections of a receding glacier, each equipped with a hook to hang the cloak and scythe, and a supply of water that burbled up from an unnatural spring. Cadets slept naked, and though chambers had an exterior shell and reapers no capacity to blush, the nudity embarrassed Cornelius.

After several hours of dormancy in a chamber, Cornelius spirited to Raleigh, North Carolina, unimpeded by remnants of a hurricane. He was anxious about the next assignment, but he dutifully arrived for Happy Hour at the DePere Restaurant & Lounge. The establishment had dark paneling and brown carpeting, a basketball game was on TV—Tarheels up by six.

Dave pulled up a stool and sat at the bar. "Evening, Valerie."

"Hi Dave."

He removed his dripping raincoat and hung it on the back of the stool, and lit a cigarette. "Bourbon and a cheeseburger...please."

"Coming right up."

Dave gulped down the bourbon, and pulled out a photo from his shirt pocket. Cornelius approached wearing a navy blue suit he lifted from a Sears in Sanford. "Great car," he said, pretending to sip his beer.

"Thanks, it's a '48 Impala," said Dave, holding up the picture. He smiled proudly. "That's my fourteen year-old daughter Annie pretending to drive." He ate a pretzel from a bowl. "I got hold of chrome lights, and paid a guy to paint duel white stripes over scratches on the hood."

"Nice."

Valerie returned with the cheeseburger.

"What do you do for a living?" Cornelius asked.

"I'm in the fast food industry," said Dave. "I work out of the corporate office as head of security." He bit into the cheeseburger and gestured to Valerie for a bottle of ketchup. "Anyway, I inspect food suppliers. Last week I was in Idaho posing as a buyer."

"Is that right?"

"Lots of farmers cheat on commercial orders." Dave removed a slice of pickle from the bun. "We have high standards. I caught a crew putting plain old potatoes in bags labeled Idaho No. 1."

"Interesting." The deception surrounding potatoes confused Cornelius.

"Can I buy you a drink?"

"No, I've got to go."

"Suit yourself."

Cornelius walked out and spirited to the passenger seat of the Impala to read over the details of the biographical scroll. Ten minutes passed before Dave exited the restaurant and started the car. The rain had changed to wet snow, and the wipers strained to keep the windshield clear. Driving home, winding around the narrow, unlit roads of McGregor Downs, Dave reached over to get a flask from the glove compartment. At that instant Cornelius caused the Impala to swerve and hit a pedestrian. Dave stopped and jumped out of the car. The chrome bumper held the limp body of a girl, and the dual white stripes were mottled with blood. He stared at the distorted face and dangling ponytail. It was Annie. "Oh God, no!" cried Dave, before collapsing dead of a heart attack.

Though adeptly managed, the Event left Cornelius heartsick. He departed the scene afraid he had made a grave mistake when he joined the cadets.

2

The sun rose over the Dwelling. It startled Cornelius out of a dormancy troubled by Residual Images. He usually dreamt of plowing the farm or picking apples from the orchard, but last night he had one about a fire, the memory of it was vague. He jumped out of the chamber and drank Universal Elixir. Clean water was the sole requirement of the reaper body. No oxygen. No calories. The body lacked the sense of taste, but it possessed touch and impeccable auditory, olfactory, and visual capabilities. It simply required dormant periods to restore its powers. Most incredibly, the body of a Grim Reaper was capable of adopting an incorporeal state and existing as an apparition, allowing a reaper to *spirit* from place to place around the world.

The supernatural body provided Grim Reapers with a physical exterior to use on a routine basis; reapers were still visible as a skeleton at the instant they reaped a soul. When among the living, reapers feigned human needs and frailties. Cadets were trained to "eat" by chewing food and then pocketing it in a cheek. They practiced coughing and sneezing, were drilled to squint at smoke and sun glare, and to blink during conversations. The use of a body originated from the need to help cadets adapt, but was extended throughout The Society of Death by popular demand, with one stipulation: a reaper was affixed with the appearance he possessed a *nanosecond* before he died. Cornelius, recruited at twenty one by smoke inhalation, retained his tall, lean body and dark brown hair filled with cowlicks. He was shocked at the state of some GRs. One had leprosy when harvested and functioned without a nose. Only naïve cadets believed the story about a headless reaper, who as a mortal was a controversial French author. He was technically still alive one nanosecond after being guillotined and therefore obligated to function as a reaper while holding his bald head by its beard.

A cold front passed over the Dwelling; strong gusts blew across its bleak landscape of rock and scrub, snow and ice. Alone, Cornelius raised the cloak high allowing the wind to blow away accumulated dust. He tried to recreate the billow of the hood, but it was baggy, a standard-issue cloak. He pulled it over his head and went to work on the blade of the scythe, using a rock as a whetstone to hone the edge. Next, he tested the handle by swinging it as if cutting wheat until satisfied the wood still had life.

Restless, he rehearsed a list of contemporary slang and colloquialisms—over three hundred commonly used words and expressions of modern America. It was important, he was told, to understand the "native tongue" and to soften the Scotch-Irish accent he retained from colonial times. He practiced S through Z, and then pocketed the list, anxious to get to the next assignment, scheduled at precisely 11:21 ante meridiem, Eastern Standard Time. Low-lying clouds and fog would slow the trip to North America. He spirited upward, identifying the clouds as stratocumuli, proud to remember the classification he learned from Linnaeus at the Replanting Department.

Cornelius drifted over the Long Island Sound, cognizant of the danger—saltwater was lethal to Grim Reapers, and the only source of pain. There was no official explanation, but the conventional wisdom was saltwater gave the Triumvirate a means of disposing of incompetent GRs. He headed to Hartford, Connecticut. As he flew over the busy streets of the city, Cornelius considered visiting the Mark Twain House and Museum—he wanted to roam the halls—but there was work to do, and he came to a barbershop on Asylum Avenue. It had two old-fashioned chairs and portraits of models with hairstyles long out of fashion. The elderly barber, Joe Poleshuk, had seventeen minutes to live. Joe draped a young boy with the flair of a magician and smiled when he requested a "crude cut" instead of a crew cut.

The electric clipper worked fast. The mother paid and the boy took a lollipop from a bowl. Joe grabbed up a broom and swept up the clumps of hair. He hummed *Singin' in the Rain* as he worked; unaware it was to be his requiem. As Cornelius placed the tip of the scythe blade on Joe, he caught a glimpse of himself in the mirror. The skeletal reflection so frightened Cornelius that he jumped and accidentally pushed Joe straight down onto the spike of a vintage cast iron receipt holder, piercing his left cheek and spewing blood across the countertop.

Jarred by the site, Cornelius left the barbershop seeking a diversion, and rode invisibly with a woman driving a gas scooter. After ten minutes of bumper-to-bumper traffic, he spirited to Hartford Hospital and the Bliss 9 ICU.

"Please try to sit up," said Susan, an aide.

Toni sat at the side of the bed, but laid back down complaining of exhaustion. Susan turned to dip a washcloth into a basin of soapy water. Cornelius moved toward Toni and completed the job. He believed the death was a merciful act, until he overheard a conversation between two tearful nurses.

"What happened? Toni was doing so much better."

"I don't know, the doctors said she had turned a corner."

Turned a corner. Cornelius felt horrible. He wanted to hide, but he was expected in Cuba. He stood on a window ledge of the hospital and leapt, spiriting south.

"Welcome." Ayodele had a high voice, unexpected with his imposing physique of 6'7".

"Hello, Master," mumbled Cornelius, awed by the illustrious Grim Reaper.

As they walked about the Old Square of Havana, Cornelius savored the scents of the unfamiliar cuisine, as always, frustrated by the inability to eat. Ayodele suggested they go over to the Castillo del Morro, explaining its use as a navigational landmark by both mortals and reapers. They came to rest on a knoll next to a row of cannons that long ago protected the harbor.

"We're waiting for Kanakuk of the Great Lakes Sector." Ayodele pulled back the sleeve of his stylish cloak and peeked at the Deco Noir wristwatch he acquired from an investment banker at the Frankfurt Stock Exchange.

"I admire your cloak, Master," commented Cornelius. Ayodele wore a custom-fitted cloak, adorned with epaulets made of cubic zirconia, an idea he got years ago when he called on the Chief Justice of the U.S. Supreme Court, William Rehnquist.

"Thank you," said Ayodele. They bounded to an alley and walked out to the street, maintaining invisibility. "Cornelius, I summoned you to Cuba because I noticed you have yet to conduct an SMR."

Systematic Multiple Reapings terrified Cornelius. SMRs required a reaper to procure at least five souls with one Event. He rubbed a piece of ivory he kept in a secret pocket and admired the immense scythe of the Master. Etched on the blade were ravens, a tribute to Edgar Allan

Poe. Ayodele boasted of owning an original poem about a reaper dictated by the famous author as he lay dying in a Baltimore hospital.

"Is it fair to say you were scarred by the Great Fire?" Ayodele asked, with a sly grin. Cornelius looked down, forever burdened with accidentally starting the Great Fire of London and causing unscheduled deaths. Ayodele lowered his hood, revealing a head full of gray stubble. "You must learn how to use Systematic Multiple Reapings." An antiquated Greyhound bus rode over a puddle, splattering mud over a few irate pedestrians.

"I attended a sea battle during the Second Anglo-Dutch War," offered Cornelius.

"The Battle of Lowestoft," clarified Ayodele. "And you were observing."

"Yes, sir."

"You will benefit from a demonstration..."

They were interrupted by the arrival of Kanakuk, a wizened man with high cheek bones and dark eyes, a descendent of a long line of Kickapoo warriors. He bowed to Ayodele but sneered at Cornelius, revealing teeth chiseled to sharp points.

They floated over to Calle Obispo. Street musicians were playing maracas, acoustic guitars and singing Cuban folk songs. Kanakuk ruined the sunny tropical morning when he pointed a long index finger—it seemed to have an extra metacarpal—toward an intersection of roads and caused a Chevrolet to collide with a horse-drawn carriage. The crash killed the drivers and passengers of both the carriage and the Chevrolet instantly, except for one woman. The horse trotted away unharmed. The power to point and cause death required decades of dedication and practice. It demanded focus, any hesitation and it failed. As the last requirement of a cadet, it elevated Kanakuk to the 3rd Tier.

"Congratulations!" Ayodele turned to face Kanakuk. "The Event you have executed completes your cadet training."

Kanakuk held his scythe high, and yelled a mysterious war cry. Cornelius wanted to hide when Ayodele applauded with the silent clapping of a reaper.

The trio hovered over the crash scene. Ayodele gestured to a deflated tire on the Chevrolet. "Superb, Kanakuk, meticulous and swift."

"Thank you, Master." Kanakuk bowed.

"We will leave you to complete your work." Ayodele led Cornelius past the lone survivor writhing and moaning from multiple fractures, a recipient of an Excruciating Death. They walked toward a beach. "Tell me, Cornelius, what have you learned about SMRs?"

"It's important to have a plan, and to keep it simple."

"What else?"

"Um, precision."

"Very good," said Ayodele.

Cornelius wanted to ask how the crude instrument of an SMR coexisted with the specificity of The Book of Expiration Dates, but instead he changed the subject. "Master, have you ever had an Allowance to Act Mortal?"

"Allowances are primarily for cadets and 3rd Tiers. It eases the transition to reaper, but it must be earned." They headed back to town and strolled past a cinema advertising the Havana Film Festival.

"Master, may I ask how old you are?"

"I was born in Ethiopia in the fifth century, and recruited as an old man."

"Do you ever have Residual Images of your life?" Cornelius immediately regretted the question—definitely inappropriate, possibly subversive.

Ayodele stopped. "Why do you ask?"

"No reason, Master." Cornelius squirmed.

"Tell me, do *you* have Residual Images?"

"No, sir," said Cornelius, lying. He had images about his life on a daily basis.

"Very well, I will visit with you again soon." Ayodele gazed sternly at Cornelius. "Make use of the lessons you learned here today. Farewell."

Cornelius was born during the autumn of 1644. He had a literate father, learned enough to help the Reverend John Eliot translate the Bible to the Algonquian language, and a well-respected mother who worked as a midwife throughout the province. When he was a boy the family moved from Boston to the Praying Town of Natick. The town was made up of natives who had converted to Christianity, part of a defensive ring around Boston to protect against hostile tribes.

Growing up, Cornelius loved hard work. He cut hay out of tall grass and squared timber for houses. After he inherited a small farm he ignored the town elders' talk of "improving" the land and instead used the more effective native farming techniques: growing corn and cultivating bean vines to climb up the stalks, and planting squash and pumpkin together on the ground so the broad leaves deterred foragers.

Cornelius was ten years dead and working at the Replanting Department when war came to New England. Metacomet, Grand Sachem of the Wampanoag, led the native tribes against the colonists throughout Massachusetts, Rhode Island and Connecticut. The conflict led colonial authorities to relocate the "Praying Indians" of Natick to Deer Island in Boston Harbor, and the vast majority died from exposure and starvation.

Cornelius remembered how demoralized he felt at learning of the injustice. The victims were admirable people, yet they suffered Systematic Multiple Reapings and Excruciating Deaths, while most of the advocates of the cruel policy lived long lives. Then, and now, he found the grotesquely unfair application of death hard to reconcile.

3

Cornelius rode the draft made by Páll as they spirited towards North America and MetLife Stadium in the New Jersey Meadowlands. He was ordered to attend the exhibition soccer game with 1st Tier/Associate Páll, special instructor to cadets and lecturer on reaperlore. LaGuardia and Newark airports were busy with departures and arrivals, and as they passed over Manhattan by the George Washington Bridge, a helicopter landed on a rooftop helipad of a hotel. Cornelius scanned the terrain, but he saw no meadows, just bugs swarming around the stadium lights.

The game was sold-out, but accessibility was the universal privilege of reapers, and Cornelius and Páll settled on the players' bench while the athletes and coaches stood on the sidelines during the national anthem of each team's country. As the game advanced, Páll guided Cornelius to the top of a guard rail on the main level, adjacent to the seats of a young couple holding hands. Nelson and Tana of Newark stayed together, huddled against the unruly, inebriated crowd.

A few minutes into the second half, eighty thousand spectators saw the Bulgarian striker score against Argentina. The crowd roared, and Tana leaned against Nelson and suggested they get "some fresh air." Páll and Cornelius followed them as they burrowed through the crowd and made it to the relative quiet of the concourse.

Tana kissed Nelson. "I love you."

"I...I...I...love y...y...you."

After respective visits to overworked restrooms, they met at a corner farthest removed from the overhead speakers and the histrionic calls of the stadium announcer.

"Are you...h...h...hungry?"

"Just a decaf, honey." Caffeine made it hard for Tana to listen to the stutter.

Nelson went to the concession stand and returned with a cup of decaffeinated coffee and a bag of peanuts.

"Wha...Wha...Wha...sc...sc...ore?"

"No change, one-nil."

Nelson and Tana walked around the concourse and settled next to a wall-sized map of the stadium. They watched the end of the game on a television monitor. Nelson ate peanuts and piled the shells atop a ledge. He kissed Tana.

"Yuck, you've got peanut breath," she said.

He pointed at Tana. "You've...g...got...p...p...p...penis breath."

Páll escorted Cornelius to the top of a long steel ventilation pipe. While Nelson and Tana improvised the

Argentine Tango, Páll knocked over the peanut shells from the ledge down to the lower concourse. Cornelius was uneasy about the impending Event as hundreds of fans formed a bulge at an exit.

Within moments, violence stirred the crowd as a group of five men kicked one man repeatedly and he bled across the cement floor. Noise from the exiting fans and the blare of vuvuzelas leftover from the World Cup muffled the sick laughter of the gang and the cries of the victim.

The perpetrators ran away at the sound of a police whistle. An officer arrived on the scene. He radioed for an ambulance and crouched down next to the man, but retracted when the victim spit up a viscous mass. Tana and Nelson rode the escalator down and overheard a witness tell the guard how the gang attacked the man when he laughed as peanut shells rained down on their heads. Páll guided Cornelius down to the incapacitated mortal. "Have I improved your understanding of an Excruciating Death?"

"Yes, sir."

"Excellent." Páll instructed Cornelius to monitor the young man, and rocketed up to a gray cloud.

The ambulance arrived, and Cornelius sat next to the stretcher and watched as paramedics urgently tended to the man, one came across a student ID card from the International Foods Institute. "Noel, stay with us, we're almost at the hospital." Although Noel survived the ride, he died on the gurney as it was rolled into the operating room.

The death upset Cornelius. What was its purpose? He wanted an explanation; surely a higher purpose justified Excruciating Deaths. He decided to visit the only reaper he trusted.

A rumor circulated that the Replanting Department was going to move out of the Krubera Cave because a team of speleologists, relying on technologically advanced equipment, recently came in striking distance of the ancient office. Linnaeus voiced a desire to relocate the RD from its present home in Abkhazia on the eastern coast of the Black Sea to the Amazon rainforest. Famed 1st Tier Roger Mortimer had recommended Howland Island in the Pacific Ocean, after noting years earlier the isolation of the island when he caused Amelia Earhart to crash.

The current office of the RD compelled a reaper to transverse a terrifying passage of dark spaces and narrow slits of dripping mud. When promoted to cadet, Cornelius resolved to avoid Krubera Cave, but he grudgingly made the trip to talk to Linnaeus. He paused at the vestibule, reluctant to disturb the overloaded team, and reconsidered the visit when the limestone door slid away.

"Welcome to our subterranean workplace!" announced Linnaeus.

"Hello, my friend." Cornelius clumsily retrieved a bag of handmade dominoes from his pocket; possessions were illegal, but enforcement lax. "Here, these are for you."

"A gift!" Linnaeus peeked into the bag. "Ah, very handsome tiles, wonderful. Thank you."

"You're welcome."

"H_2O?" Linnaeus asked, filling a cup from a pitcher—both made from the clay in the cave.

"Yes, please."

Linnaeus carefully examined the individual dominos. Cornelius had carved images of plants and animals on the back of each tile, and smiled watching the legendary taxonomist organize the set into a three-dimensional classification chart. He imagined Linnaeus meandering around the old Natick farm, wearing a big straw hat and talking about the plants and animals of Massachusetts.

"You've depicted the flora and fauna magnificently." Linnaeus smiled at the tile with the image of a platypus. "Do you want to play a game of tiddly-wink?"

"No, I have to get back to the Dwelling."

"Already? You've braved Krubera, stay awhile."

Cornelius halfheartedly followed Linnaeus across the threshold of the office. Anticipating the cramped interior with its torches and reams of biographical scrolls, he was surprised by its complete overhaul: a soft glow radiated from ramekins burning mysterious oil, six limestone drafting tables replaced one rough square table and scrolls were alphabetized on shelves chiseled out of the wall. "You've really improved the place."

"Thank you," said Linnaeus. He turned when a Team Member came over to the door.

"I beg your pardon," said Russell, GR-RD/3. "I have an appointment with the Great Spirit of the Mata Mata." Cornelius felt immensely relieved to be free of such meetings.

"Very well," said Linnaeus. "Enjoy your trip to South America. No delays, return promptly."

"Of course, sir." Russell stepped past the threshold and spirited out of the cave.

"Cornelius, my friend," said Linnaeus, "I cherish the dominoes, but I presume you have another reason for visiting."

"Yes, I have a question."

"I am at your service."

Cornelius lowered the hood of his cloak. "Why do some people receive Excruciating Deaths?"

"Shh!" Linnaeus looked around as if expecting a 1st Tier to materialize. He gestured to Cornelius to step back to the vestibule. "No Grim Reaper understands the basis of determining an Excruciating Death. The judgments are allegedly made by the Triumvirate."

"Allegedly?" Cornelius wanted an explanation, not a controversy, and decided against asking about the workings of Systematic Multiple Reapings.

"1st Tiers supposedly receive the assignments regarding Excruciating Deaths from the Triumvirate."

"I'm confused," said Cornelius, agitated by the vague response.

Linnaeus paced. "The answer to your question is a question: Why are specific mortals selected to receive an Excruciating Death? I suggest we apply the scientific method."

"The scientific method?" Cornelius wanted a simple answer.

"The scientific method is useful when confronted with an unknown. I suggest we formulate a hypothesis: An inordinate number of enlightened souls have received an Excruciating Death."

"Okay."

"Next we conduct research." Linnaeus explained how they would have to examine past Excruciating Deaths to validate the question.

"But I saw a man at a soccer game…"

"Wait." Linnaeus held up both hands. "Follow the method. We will test our hypothesis and analyze the results. If wicked souls have received nearly all of the Excruciating Deaths, our hypothesis was wrong." He peered up at the infinite dark cavities of the Krubera Cave. "On the other hand, if a disproportionate number of Excruciating Deaths were bestowed upon enlightened mortals…"

"It means our hypothesis was right?" Cornelius asked, tentatively.

DEATH of a GRIM REAPER

Linnaeus turned away, avoiding eye contact.

"What?"

"Nothing, nothing," said Linnaeus. He suggested Cornelius get back to the important duties of a cadet and abruptly bid farewell. Paranoid about the conversation, Cornelius hurried out of Krubera Cave and headed back to North America.

There were blue skies and a daytime moon over the eastern seaboard of the United States as Cornelius approached New York. He treasured the ability to spirit, but flew cautiously, staying under the speed limit of 43.4 knots. Typically, cadets were intoxicated by flight, and flew around mountains and canyons and over lakes and jungles, and visited places of historical significance such as religious sites and ancient ruins. A number were prideful about spiriting and competed over velocity, agility, and daring, but competitions were outlawed when a promising cadet perished by accidentally touching saltwater during a race through the barrel of an ocean wave.

Cornelius headed north over the Hudson River, and slowed down over Lake Tear of the Clouds in the Adirondack Mountains. He remembered rowing down the Charles River as a teenager, and decided to sail down the Hudson on a piece of driftwood. He abandoned the vessel and went to explore the Clermont Manor, but hid when he unexpectedly saw Kanakuk holding a scythe over a park ranger leading a tour. The upstate region of New York contained overlapping GR districts as a result of centuries of shifting Native American communities. Cornelius wanted to avoid the new 3rd Tier and returned to the river.

The sunshine and fresh air alleviated some of his anxiety. He moved to a barge and coasted. When it reached the Upper New York Bay, Cornelius heeded the advice to avoid the river as it mixed with saltwater and floated to the top of the George Washington Bridge. The view of the Manhattan skyline was spectacular. The violent winds atop the bridge buffeted Cornelius. He faced the truth: Linnaeus was wrong; no research was required to know that most Excruciating Deaths were unjustified.

Later, back at the Dwelling, Cornelius sat carving the tusk of a walrus. Carving killed time. He obtained the ivory tusk on an assignment to acquire the soul of Anuun, an Inuit man from the lower Canadian Arctic. Anuun had shot a walrus with a bow and arrow and as he came up to remove its tusks with a knife the creature stirred, and with a last gasp lurched at the hunter. Cornelius had repositioned the knife so that the blade fatally cut Anuun, and remembered how the man smiled at the beauty of the aurora borealis as he bled out.

Cornelius worked on the tusk. He wanted to sculpt the head of Arabella, a gray mare he once owned, but struggled with an improvised chisel made of rock. He loved that draft horse and wished he was back on the farm. There was no love as a reaper, only death.

4

Reaperkind was at its zenith during the Dark Ages. Mortals were weak. There was no real judicial system, so it was easy to get a mortal convicted of a crime and executed, physicians of the day only hastened death, and widespread food shortages put whole populations at risk. Whether it was a soldier on a battlefield, or a woman straining to give birth, death was easy. If a serf glimpsed the shadow of the cloaked silhouette holding a scythe, he immediately fell over dead, or if a parishioner saw a reaper staring down from the altar, gesturing to come with a skeletal hand, he accepted fate. Human beings lived and some loved, but the vast majority died at the touch of a Grim Reaper, only a statistically insignificant few died from natural causes or genuine accidents.

Now, the power of reapers was on the decline. Most Grim Reapers blamed technology. There were instances of failed reapings such as a recent one involving an Indian computer technician who was test-driving a BMW in New Delhi (young male drivers were considered easy assignments). As the mortal sped past a construction site, he skidded and crashed into a parked cement truck. During the Event, the overconfident cadet imprudently sat in the backseat of the car. The airbag deployed on impact and the driver survived, retaining a vague memory of "a man wearing a cloak." The cadet was guilty of a Sighting, and as a result, reassigned as a Caretaker with the tedious job of monitoring brain dead mortals.

An increasing number of reapers viewed technology as an existential threat and advocated drastic measures, specifically stealing the souls of inventors, innovators, and scientists, but the concept was unpalatable to the majority and impossible to implement without damaging the basic tenets of The Society of Death.

Prior to the invention of the printing press by Guttenberg, most mortals had no impact on The Divine Trajectory of Life and souls were routinely harvested in bundles. However, the invention of moveable type—technology—spread learning to the masses and reduced the number of inconsequential mortals and made bundling obsolete.

Modern forensic science further complicated death. Last year a reaper spilled residual volcanic ash on his cloak while on assignment in Iowa, causing local police to launch an investigation. While inconclusive, the inquiry stirred enough unease to impose penalties on the culpable GR.

The invention of photography caused *permanent* Sightings, evident by the vague images of the Grim Reaper in various battlefield photos of the American Civil War. Digital photography exacerbated the issue, increasing the odds of clear, unmistakable Sightings.

Ayodele scheduled a meeting to address the "gathering storm" of technology on a chunk of ice about the size of a school bus floating by the South Pole. Every Grim Reaper Cadet assigned to North America was in attendance:

Tristan, originally from Canada, was assigned to Texas, a limited geographical area but with a high number of reapings. The young cadet had scars on both cheeks resembling the coagulated top of leftover gravy as a result of third-degree burns suffered at the instant of recruitment. He repeatedly expressed a desire to conduct Excruciating Deaths.

Javier was recruited by gunshot, and had a bullet hole in the back of the head which he concealed with a tuft of hair. He had a mortal background as a sex trafficker, and as the rare cadet who had no qualms about reaping children, he was tasked with raising infant and child mortality in the southwestern United States and northern Mexico.

Levi Anderson, a retired insurance salesman, died of complications from diabetes and lost a leg to the disease, he wore a prosthetic when moving among the living. He received special training to facilitate an experimental form of SMRs in the Mountain Time Zone of North America, specifically, manipulating selected mortals to act as "catalysts", including arsonists, serial killers, gun runners, and drug kingpins.

Kao, twenty five years-old when recruited from Japan in 1971 and assigned to the west coast of North America, stood at the edge of the ice as if to stare down the ocean. Judged the highest rated cadet, he received a private Dwelling atop Mount Fuji in recognition of maintaining a perfect record of reapings. Kao had a slender build, angular features, and a somber countenance. He was fast approaching promotion, and indications were that he would bypass the 3rd Tier and move directly to the 2nd.

Cornelius walked over to the burly Skowron, originally from Arch Cape, Oregon, but assigned to the Central North American District. He was reaped by drowning and had a blue complexion.

"Hi, how are you, pal?" Skowron asked.

"Okay." Cornelius felt almost human when talking to the avuncular Skowron. "How are things in Kansas and Missouri?"

"Flat." Skowron shrugged. "I miss the ocean."

They turned when Ayodele materialized and called the cadets to attention. He inspected each one as if he were a drill sergeant and reiterated the warning to be vigilant when spiriting in a corporeal state (suspending invisibility conserved energy). Ayodele glanced up at a squall, snowflakes dusted the reapers. As he discussed the danger posed by technologically sophisticated cameras, he removed a scroll from his sleeve and unfurled it. "Today,

I have the solemn honor to deliver a new edict by the esteemed 1st Tier Alvarez."

Each cadet advanced toward the wrinkled parchment, except Javier, who blithely ignored it. Levi analyzed it as meticulously as a lawyer, and Tristan ran a finger over each line as he read. Cornelius noticed Skowron seemed to wilt when he read the scroll.

The last paragraph of the proclamation stated unambiguously:

...For the punishment does not take place for the correction of the guilty, but for the good of The Society of Death...thus each individual Grim Reaper will be terrified and avoid committing a Sighting...

The cadets waited silently. Customarily, the importance of a proclamation was emphasized by a lethal demonstration. Ayodele produced a copy of the *St. Louis Post-Dispatch* and opened up to a page with a grainy image of a tractor-trailer accident. Visible over the shoulder of a police officer was the face of Skowron within the hood of a cloak.

Ayodele turned to Skowron. "Grim Reaper Cadet, you were guilty of a Sighting." Skowron swayed, almost felled by the knowledge he would receive the ultimate punishment: Expulsion. Cornelius wanted to protest that the punishment was unfair. No reaper had received a sentence of Expulsion in over four centuries. The last instance involved a Grim Reaper who refused to conduct an Excruciating Death on a Franciscan friar with unique cosmological views. In the end, the friar burned at the stake with the assistance of Roger Mortimer, and the insubordinate reaper was pushed off the cliffs of Polignano a Mare to the saltwater of the Adriatic Sea.

"Your scythe and cloak," demanded Ayodele.

Skowron complied and Ayodele lowered the cloak and scythe into the ocean, both liquefied on contact. Frightened, Cornelius wondered if *he* was guilty of a Sighting.

Ayodele pointed at Skowron and the round-shouldered, unfit body chipped and peeled, bit by bit revealing the skeleton, still identifiable as Skowron by the barrel chest caused by oversized ribs. He walked haltingly to the edge of the ice and stepped off, submerging under the water. Dark suds bubbled to the surface. Skowron was expelled.

Ayodele hovered over the cadets and warned: "Remember...No Sightings!"

After the Master vanished, the group loitered, but as waves spilled over the sides of the ice floe, Levi urgently recommended that a return to work was, "the proper thing to do." One by one the cadets departed.

Kao approached Cornelius. "Very draconian."

"Huh?"

"The punishment," said Kao. "In my estimation, it was extremely unfair to expel a fine cadet over such an inconsequential Sighting."

Cornelius ignored Kao. He was angry at Ayodele. The Master appeared as dignified as a magistrate, but he was an executioner.

"What do you think?" Kao asked.

Cornelius frowned. "What's the difference?"

"You have no opinion?"

"Sure I do," he said. "But why do you care?"

Kao bowed slightly, and spirited away.

Cornelius walked to the edge of the ice. "Goodbye, Skowron."

5

Roger Mortimer was a distinguished 1st Tier Grim Reaper with a long list of accomplishments.

He boasted of reaping Nicolaus Copernicus and a hundred years later Galileo Galilei by the classic method—holding the scythe high and pointing an index finger to stop the heart. Mortimer felt a rush of power whenever he plucked the soul of a genius or a national leader. He possessed superior hand-eye coordination and memorably helped a pathetic assassin aim a rifle at a presidential motorcade; he regretted that the death of President Kennedy failed to produce a war between the United Sates and the Soviet Union.

Aggrieved by technology, Mortimer eagerly harvested the souls of space explorers. He was proud of reaping the crew of Apollo 1 by causing a fire in the capsule. He received accolades for the stylish deaths of the crew of the space shuttle Challenger, and acted as a consultant to 1st Tier Sergei Trotkov regarding the deaths of cosmonauts.

A bright Floridian morning was ideal weather for the inaugural flight of the NASA SpaceJet *Pioneer*. The excitement surrounding the launch was evident from the crowds at the viewing locations of the Cape Canaveral Air Force Station, and from the vast assemblage of media from around the world.

The *Pioneer* was the next generation of reusable space transport vehicle following the space shuttle. The contours of its body resembled a private jet, and the *Pioneer* would eventually accommodate twenty passengers. It would offer old-fashioned services with flight attendants, and its exorbitant ticket prices were expected to drop. The construction of the SpaceJet created thousands of high-paying hi-tech jobs in Florida and gave the administration of President Rose Carson a major triumph to boast of at the next election. The enthusiastic support of the country rivaled the early days of the space program. Many talking heads criticized the SpaceJet as a boondoggle, and comedians poked fun at the cost overruns, but most heralded the prospect of space tourism and speculated on the possibility of space resorts.

A chance to dash the dreams of mortalkind was ambrosia to Mortimer. Excited by the prospect of ripping out the souls of astronauts Kartalian and Wagner, Mortimer passed over their heads as they boarded the SpaceJet. The Book of Expiration Dates indicated both were scheduled to die at 11:23 when the *Pioneer* would be orbiting Earth. Imagining the Event seen by the whole world—living and dead—invigorated Mortimer.

The two pilots surveyed the cockpit and sat at the control board to run a systems check. A scheduled interview was imminent, so they put on the crisp uniform jackets of white and teal, emphasizing their clean-cut appearance. NASA understood that budgets were linked to public support and that telegenic astronauts were good for business. A barely visible camera on the consul came to life with a hum and alerted the pilots they were on live television.

"Welcome aboard the *Pioneer*. I'm Captain Lou Wagner. Please allow me to introduce my navigator, Commander Don Kartalian."

"Hi, everybody," said Kartalian with a wave. "It's a great day for a test-flight."

After several minutes of banter with an unctuous television host, and an obligatory call from President Carson, the light of the camera went out; a camera outside the *Pioneer* would send high-definition images of the galaxy back to Earth.

The astronauts removed their NASA uniform jackets to reveal T-shirts depicting the SpaceJet as an intergalactic bottle of Jack Daniels. They maneuvered the *Pioneer* into position. There was no countdown; liftoff was equivalent to the take-off of an airplane, without the delays. The SpaceJet raced down the runway, cheers were audible from mission control and Wagner and Kartalian celebrated with high-fives.

Mortimer stood next to the payload operations panel, tempted to materialize and reduce the self-assured astronauts to quivering masses. He moved toward Wagner and Kartalian, almost mad with anticipation, but it was not yet time.

"Mission control, we have achieved orbit," relayed Captain Wagner.

"I copy that," responded the flight controller. "Contact us when you're over the Indian Ocean."

"Copy." Captain Wagner turned to Kartalian. "Buck?"

"Aye, captain?"

"Did you remember to go to the bathroom?"

"Damn it, I knew I forgot something."

Their laughter stopped when part of the control board went dark. The *Pioneer* drifted. Wagner and Kartalian moved swiftly, manipulating an array of buttons and switches and calmly restoring control over the SpaceJet. Mortimer approved of the courage displayed by the mortals. They would have made excellent knights.

Wagner set the SpaceJet on auto-pilot, and he and Kartalian moved to a zero-gravity area of the cabin devoted to research. It reduced costs and criticism of the *Pioneer*. They initiated a simple experiment to test a device with the potential to offer superior analysis of a drug that showed promise as a cure for cancer.

Mortimer glanced out a window, stunned by the view. Undeterred by the majesty of the world, he stood at the control board, ready to flip the switch to activate the parachute used during landings to decelerate the vehicle. He understood enough to commit sabotage, and knew that premature release of the parachute would cause a radical shift in the trajectory of the *Pioneer*. He expected the pilots to suffer extreme trauma and have no chance to pull out of the tailspin. The crash would be magnificent and reaperkind would marvel at the Event. Glory was as vital to Mortimer as Universal Elixir.

He extended the right index finger—it had terminated an incalculable number of lives over the centuries. Mortimer relished the impending catastrophe, but as he attempted to flip the switch to release the parachute, the reliable digit glided over the lever as if it were a hologram.

Mortimer ricocheted around the cabin of the SpaceJet, indiscriminately hitting instruments to no avail. He last panicked seven hundred years ago when arrested at Nottingham Castle by soldiers and hauled to the Tower of London. The venomous memory of the pain of hanging gave him the idea to try and choke Wagner, but the captain kept working, unfazed.

Mortimer stumbled backward and slumped down to the floor. According to The Book of Expiration Dates the astronauts should be dead. How was it they were still alive? The *Pioneer* cruised above the atmosphere. Mortimer peered out at the empty universe, wondering if he was sick, he had heard rumors of reapers suffering mysterious ailments. As the SpaceJet traveled over Africa, he realized reaper power was confined to Earth. The revelation was almost unbearable.

He returned to Cape Canaveral, and impulsively insti-gated a seven car pile-up on Route 528. Pacified for the moment by the screams and gore, Mortimer spirited away.

Back in the 14th century, Mortimer was as an English nobleman—Roger de Mortimer, 3rd Baron Mortimer, 1st Earl of March. He had an aquiline nose and piercing blue eyes, and an unquenchable urge to rule. Conspiratorial by nature, he bred rivals. In due course, Mortimer was arrested on trumped-up charges, but he bribed prison guards and escaped the Tower of London and fled to Europe vowing revenge.

In 1326 Mortimer invaded England and dethroned King Edward II. He ruled as Regent, living luxuriously at Nottingham Castle and appropriating wealthy estates with no regard for the law. Everything changed on a cold and damp evening in 1330 when a cohort loyal to the young heir Edward III captured Mortimer. He was dragged to the gallows, stripped of the emerald and gold silk uniform of the elite military unit he commanded—it was wrapped around a pig, and pelted by spectators with rotten food and rocks. The soldiers hung Mortimer by a short drop to prolong his agony. An Excruciating Death of twenty nine minutes' duration.

The limitation of reaper power to Earth, as demon-strated by the unsuccessful Event aboard the SpaceJet

Pioneer, impacted every Grim Reaper. Nearly all accepted the news, given 99.999999% of mortals were fixed to the Earth. One overwrought GR predicted that one day mortals would live among the stars and render reapers obsolete, a vestigial part of the universe.

Meanwhile, the faction known as the Provocateurs wanted Mortimer reprimanded for causing unscheduled reapings on Route 528 in Florida. Also, they claimed he was guilty of a Sighting on the *Pioneer* as the extreme cold of a reaper body created a temperature variation outlined as a human body on a thermal assessment at mission control. They revived an old peccadillo Mortimer committed years ago at a showing of *Robin Hood* at Carlsbad Caverns when he became upset over the depiction of Nottingham Castle and yelled at Ayodele: "Damn your cinema!"

Provocateurs wanted Mortimer demoted to a position without power—one argued that he deserved Expulsion, and were disappointed when he was only barred from future assignments involving astronauts.

Mortimer was incensed by the criticism. Humiliated by the reprimand. And motivated.

Grim Reapers were taught dark energy corrupted death. It twisted and tempted reapers to act against The Divine Trajectory of Life. They were warned to guard against its insatiable appetite to devour souls. Mortimer always considered such teachings parochial and now, as he spirited up the southern coast of Ireland, he invited dark energy. He listened to its strange voice—brusque, deep, yet purely intuitive. It avowed to help Mortimer restore the power of Grim Reapers over the world. When dark energy promised *he* would rule Death, an overjoyed Mortimer raced across the Irish Sea, over the mountains of Wales and landed in the English town of Wick.

Inspired, he casually went to the backroom of a clothier and removed the attire of a smartly dressed mannequin, and walked down Coach Road to Lofton Tailors. An old shop with an odor of mildew.

Mortimer politely requested of the elderly proprietor a rush order "to fix a costume." He watched as Alice Lofton skillfully sewed emerald and gold silk into the sleeves of the cloak, a gesture to honor the old uniform.

He was pleased with cloak and handed Alice £20. A fair exchange. The mortal was a fine tailor, and the cloak was now a splendid uniform to wear while he killed millions.

6

The hook and cable of the flag pole of the Hanscom Air Force Base in Concord, Massachusetts, rattled noisily in the wind. Cornelius stared straight ahead with dry eyes. As a boy, even a breeze would make his eyes water as if he were crying and caused the other boys to tease him. It led to a lot of brawls.

He came to rest atop a parked jeep and focused on the biographical scroll of Sergeant Lyle McDonough, forty four year-old mechanic of the Massachusetts National Guard. The sergeant resented the repeated call-ups as a result of the extended missions of the United States Air Force over Burma. He suffered from a bad back and a bad marriage.

Cornelius explored an airplane hangar, astonished by the complexity of helicopters. He wondered how people learned to fly the machines, spiriting was as simple as lifting an arm or extending a leg. He remembered his maiden flight with Páll, mostly the overwhelming vertigo he experienced over the Atlantic Ocean and the beauty of the White Cliffs of Dover.

Sergeant McDonough completed routine maintenance on a V-22, and stepped outside to smoke a cigarette. At 11:08, he went to the latrine and sat on the toilet. Cornelius floated up and peeked over the stall.

"What the hell?" McDonough barked.

Unnerved, Cornelius almost dropped the scythe, before he lifted it over the wall and placed the tip on McDonough's chest, short-circuiting the electric conduction of his heart. The sergeant collapsed forward, knocking the stall door open. Cornelius wanted to fix the man's pants and flush the toilet, but he complied with reaper protocol and left the scene undisturbed.

He lingered around the base. The sun created lively shadows of swaying tree branches and reminded Cornelius of the Salem Witch Trials of 1692. The flinty 1st Tier Harbottle produced a multitude of deaths by tormenting adolescent girls with occasional moments of visibility, subsequently used as "spectral evidence" to condemn mortals to death.

Cornelius was chaperoned at the witch trials by Bu'shar, a Grim Reaper originally from Syria. He was recruited in an age when dark cloaks were optional and wore a white linen robe. During the course of the trials, Bu'shar acted as if they were merely a sporting event, alternately gossiping and chatting about the frequent visits he made home to Syria.

Cornelius finally received authorization to visit home one hundred years following recruitment. By 1765, Natick had grown to a sizeable New England town, with a fledging newspaper and a proper schoolhouse. The American Revolution stirred and he enjoyed eavesdropping on the town assembly as it debated the Stamp Act. But he was heartbroken when he realized the native tribes of the region were extinct.

The Hanscom Air Force Base was just twelve miles from Natick and he was tempted to make an unauthorized visit. The desire was powerful. It excited Cornelius, and with a playful impulse, he walked down a runway of the base with arms outstretched, pretending to be an airplane.

Unexpectedly, Páll materialized. He held up both hands to indicate stop: "I understand the attraction!"

"Excuse me?"

"The proximity of your origins acts as a magnet."

"I'm sorry, I..."

"I suggest we talk, please follow."

They flitted six miles from the base to the woods surrounding Walden Pond, and landed on a slope covered with pine needles. "I want to help you gain perspective," said Páll. He frowned at a sign about protecting the path around the lake from erosion. "Most cadets want to visit home, most have doubts."

"Really?"

"Absolutely. Even I had doubts. They originated from Residual Images of Iceland. Do you ever have images?"

"Um, no." Cornelius wanted to guard the bright Residual Images against the shadow of death.

"Might I share my experiences?"

"I would be honored," said Cornelius, details of the history of a 1st Tier was considered privileged information.

"I was born in 1541. When I came of age our climate had changed—frozen waters limited fishing, and extremely cold temperatures killed crops. We struggled to survive." Páll lowered the hood of the cloak, revealing a barely attached, mutilated left ear. It bobbed as he moved. "Anyway, I promised to wed a woman from the neighboring village...Baugheiõur had long dark hair and blue eyes."

Cornelius was riveted.

"Many times, I regretted that I was recruited. Residual Images of Baugheiõur emerging from a hot spring, wet and glistening made existence as a Grim Reaper intolerable. I wanted to go back to my village." Páll glared at a pair of mortals walking past. "But I worked hard and achieved the status of 1st Tier/Associate. If you try, you will forget about Natick...We, The Society of Death, offer you infinite possibilities."

"Yes, sir," said Cornelius, knowing he would never forget Natick.

As they walked around Walden Pond, Páll expressed how it was critical to reestablish the fear of death, and cited Henry David Thoreau as a cautionary tale because he accepted death with serenity. Páll kicked dirt over the flat stone marking the exact location of the fireplace in Thoreau's cabin.

"Ayodele and I have high expectations of you, Cornelius. We gave you the chance to leave the RD because you possess many fine qualities."

"Thank you, sir."

"I have to go, but I warn you…cast away your doubts!"

Páll lifted off the ground and spirited away. "The doubts get stronger by the day," muttered Cornelius. He walked down a trail, and watched two boys collect pinecones and wished he were a child again.

He left the park and followed Route 126. He landed on a trail with a historical sign praising the local farmers who fought the professional soldiers of Great Britain in the American Revolution. Today was a peaceful day, a father carrying a baby, a few tourists. Invisible, Cornelius crossed the old North Bridge holding the scythe as if were a rifle, pretending to march to confront the British. When he reached the Minute Man statue on the west side of Concord River, he decided to ignore the advice of Páll and visit Natick.

Immediately Cornelius regretted the visit. Natick was unrecognizable, filled with neighborhoods, tall buildings and traffic lights, and covered with pavement. He had fantasized about returning to the Natick of dirt roads and hand-built structures. He took no solace from a boulder with a plaque about John Elliot and the Praying Indians.

Almost no open land remained adjacent to the Charles River and Cornelius wondered how people managed when it overflowed its banks. He walked down a road to a stone bridge with the inscription: Pleasant Street. The river was beautiful and he recognized the surrounding rock formations, virtually unchanged except for a statue of St. Francis of Assisi standing on a boulder.

He walked down a rough-hewn trail, reflexively wary of poison ivy and thorn bushes. Cornelius wished he were alive. He walked past Lake Waban, besieged by illuminated houses. He wanted to catch a fish, collect kindling and fry it over an open fire. The path led back to streets and stores. Some roads seemed to travel age-old paths, and one led to the site of an old armory, replaced by a park with a gazebo. There was a fire station, a church and a library. The praying village had grown up. The elegant façade of the Odd Fellows' Building intrigued Cornelius, but a scrawl of unintelligible cursive painted on one wall marred the view.

When it got dark, Cornelius entered Hometown Hardware through a vent. He lifted a can of red paint, grabbed a brush and walked upstairs to the roof. He painted over the graffiti on the brick wall—undeniably a violation of the Code of Conduct, but somehow he felt safe in Natick. He relaxed on the roof and gazed up at the stars and forgot about death for awhile.

He watched the town wake up, busy with kids and crossing guards, cars and buses. He spirited back to Lake

Waban and high over the area, pinpointed a place with cultivated fields and a surrounding forest. A sign indicated it was the Natick Community Organic Farm. Cornelius had no comprehension of "organic" farming—farming was farming—but the patch of land seemed familiar. He scooped up a pile of dirt and sifted it by hand, it was full of worms. It felt good.

A woman led a group of children down a path to a pond. Cornelius smiled as the boys and girls caught frogs with hand-held nets, and remembered the time he dared a friend to juggle eggs and the boy dropped each one. The soaked children waddled back to the barn and opened a spigot to clean off the mud. Leaning on the lower half of a split-door, Cornelius watched the group sit at a picnic table and eat fresh goat cheese and bread.

When recruited, Cornelius was promised unlimited powers, but time on a farm convinced him that a regular lifespan—vibrant and true—outshined all the powers of being a Grim Reaper and existing for over a millennium. He coasted upwards and tapped a hive hanging from a branch high over the picnic table, and smiled as hornets swarmed toward the howling children. He had always loved horseplay.

Back at the Dwelling, Cornelius sat on a rock carving the tusk. It bore no resemblance to Arabella, and he considered changing it to a fish. As he carved grooves to create the mane, he imagined how he would spend a Vacation of a Lifetime; last measured at 79.32 years (average life expectancy of a Costa Rican) to honor GR Morales, credited with originating the idea in 1749. If he ever earned the privilege, Cornelius decided he would be a farmer again and grow crops and raise animals. A coarse voice shattered the respite. It was Tristan.

"What the hell are you doing?"

"What does it look like? I'm carving." Cornelius no longer remembered why they bickered. They were about the same age, and he figured they ought to be friends, or at least civil. He wondered if he had antagonized the devout cadet with an idle comment about how reapers scribbled on scrolls with quills while mortals used computers. Cornelius put the tusk down and attempted to act hospitable. "Are you returning from an assignment?"

"Yep, down in Dalhart." Tristan brushed away bits of grain from his cloak. "The mortal had climbed up on a grain elevator and I shoved him, it was a long plunge," he said, with a short laugh. "Anyway, he suffocated with a mouthful of grain."

"You're an idiot," said Cornelius, dropping hospitality.

"Yeah? You're a coward!"

"What are you talking about?"

"Everybody knows you haven't performed one Excruciating Death," asserted Tristan. "What's the matter, are you afraid?"

"I haven't gotten such an assignment."

"Excuses, excuses."

"At least I didn't try to get out of an assignment at an office building." Tristan was embarrassed when he hesitated to complete an assignment at *Texas Saltwater Fishing* when it only involved the editor of the magazine and no actual saltwater.

"What do we have here?" Tristan snatched the tusk.

"Hey, give me that."

"This is contraband." Tristan kicked the tusk as if punting a football and it landed in a snowdrift.

Cornelius swiftly retrieved the tusk, and pointed an index finger at Tristan—an obscene gesture among reapers.

"You'll regret that," said Tristan. He approached a chamber and removed the new textured, dark plum cloak he wore—it once belonged to Roger Mortimer—and stood naked, revealing a torso of unhealed, burned flesh. He stepped into the chamber, and as it shut, shouted, "I promise...I will hurt you!"

7

Cornelius sat at an oak table of a nursing home reviewing a scroll. The table functioned as the callers' station for bingo, a podium for resident council meetings, and an altar for religious services. A half-century ago the split-level house was a retreat, a place to dry-out from alcohol, and conversation at the table allegedly included the laugh and temper of Jackie Gleason and the sweet voice and regrets of Judy Garland.

Maureen, a nurse of thirty six years, pushed down the curling vinyl flooring with her left foot and crushed a black carpenter ant with the right, aggravated to have to work the Baylor shift—twelve hours Saturday and twelve Sunday. The morning routine flowed as it always had: a delivery of medical supplies, trivia questions read to a somnolent group, a trio of smokers led out to the portico to have one cigarette. Maureen doled out the morning pills, and then returned to the nursing station. The scroll informed Cornelius that Maureen was upset by the way younger staff handled residents. Last Sunday, an aide giggled as Elizabeth Bryson, a long-retired maternity nurse, opened a peanut butter and jelly sandwich to use as a trap to catch a fly.

Cornelius hated to reap Maureen at work; it would be what people remembered, and not the years of dedicated service. He wanted Maureen to walk away from the nursing station and go to a private part of the building, but assignments ignored the dignity of people. Maureen shivered from the cold and collapsed dead, falling forward, slamming against the computer screen and smashing her jaw wide open, before she slumped to the floor and her uncontrolled bowels released. Cornelius spirited away ashamed.

Following recruitment, conscripts were required to complete basic training, including a general orientation and role-playing on how to avoid detection when operating among mortals. Typically, recruits worked in an unfamiliar region in a commonplace role—such as a serf, infantryman, custodian, cashier, or taxi driver—while prohibited from meddling in mortal affairs.

When originally recruited, Cornelius was sent to England and placed as an apprentice to a baker on Pudding Lane in London. He was a good fit at the bakery. He loved the aroma of freshly baked bread, and enjoyed capturing, cleaning and dicing rabbits and pigeons to bake meat pies. The heavy work of lifting trays, stoking ovens, and hauling water was easy with a reaper body, impervious to muscle strain. During summer, Cornelius complained about the heat, and pretended to sweat by regularly dabbing water on his armpits, low back, and forehead.

The bakery was a sloppy, oversized kitchen, recognizable as a shop by a wooden sign over the door crafted to resemble a loaf of bread. Cornelius handled customers every morning as the owner slept off a hangover, and remembered one instance of handing a meat pie to a woman as two adorable children stole loaves of rye with seeds that were actually bits of tree bark. He witnessed the ugly violence of the street when he ventured to pick up bags of flour down at the pier, but he enjoyed the trips to the country to collect herbs. He wanted to visit a castle, but everything changed when he caused the Great Fire of London.

One evening, while cleaning out the oven, Cornelius somehow ignited a fire that, swept up by the wind, grew out of control. The flames spread, accelerated by the glut of buildings made of timber and packed with combustibles such as hemp, tallow, and coal. The fire devastated London. The city lost churches, guild halls, governmental buildings, and thousands of homes. The conflagration caused surprisingly few unscheduled deaths, and as no victim altered The Divine Trajectory of Life, Cornelius received the relatively lenient punishment of reassignment to the Replanting Department. The real punishment he endured was the guilt at causing unscheduled deaths, what he considered *unnecessary* deaths.

Cornelius used Cape Cod and Long Island as geographical landmarks, and moving south identified Atlantic City by its glut of casinos and hotels. He spotted Delaware Bay and followed the course of the river to the Walt Whitman Bridge and South Philadelphia; rush-hour traffic clogged the city. America of the 21st century was sure jam-packed with people, he thought, recalling that, when he was a boy, the region was the frontier, with territorial claims by the Dutch and Swedish.

The apartment building at 165 Broadhurst Gardens housed squatters and recipients of Section 8 subsidies, few tenants made rent. Litter blew west down a federally funded brick sidewalk set against the backdrop of decaying buildings. Stephen Handel kept a traveling alarm clock, blackout window shades and a mattress, but no television or furniture. The biographical scroll explained how he invited women to stay at the apartment without charging rent as part of an illicit pact. Cornelius was instructed to mete out an Excruciating Death to the mortal. He followed Stephen downtown.

Even though Cornelius wanted to prove to Páll and Ayodele that he was a capable cadet, he wanted no part of an Excruciating Death. He remembered the brutal punishments of New England—food deprivation, public shaming in the stockade, cleft sticks attached to the tongue, ducking stools over water, whippings, brandings, and hangings—and how people gawked as the transgressor suffered. Whenever possible, he would avoid the spectacle; grateful he only experienced the stockade once for sleeping late on the Sabbath. Now he was expected to be the instrument of a slow and agonizing death. Cornelius rubbed the handle of the scythe almost hard enough to reduce it to sawdust. What if he failed to administer the Excruciating Death? Maybe Tristan was right, maybe he was afraid.

Stephen scouted out street corners, convenience stores, check-cashing shops, and the bus station. At last he targeted a tall, skinny woman standing under the arch of a boarded-up church; a nor'easter had toppled its steeple and reduced it to a pile of holy pick-up sticks.

"Hey, I'm Stephen." He offered the woman a cigarette. "What's your name?"

"Barbara."

"It's cold out here," said Stephen, shivering.

"Yeah?" Barbara exhaled smoke through her nostrils. "You walked over here to talk about the damn weather?"

"Ah, no, you're right. I wanted to talk to you about a bargain."

Barbara lifted up a long piece of cardboard and nudged Tamika. "C'mon, wake up Beyoncé. We have a guest."

Tamika stood slowly. ""I'm up, I'm up."

Cornelius fidgeted, unsure of the Event. It would happen on the grounds of an old church, and he imagined a scolding from the Reverend John Elliot. Stephen patted each pocket, trying to find a joint, but Cornelius had removed it to disrupt the routine of the "bargain." Stephen explained the parameters of a deal to exchange a clean, warm apartment for sex on demand, when without warning Tamika plunged a knife into Stephen. He stumbled over a car battery, coughed up blood, and collapsed.

Cornelius was consumed by guilt over whispering to the drug addled Tamika: "Kill the man, or he will kill you." He watched a curdled soul depart the body of Stephen Handel, when suddenly he was joined by Ayodele and ordered to spirit to an alley filled with damaged shopping carts. They materialized safely out of view from the street.

"That was hardly an Excruciating Death," Ayodele scolded. "It measured only 14.8 seconds!"

Cornelius wanted to complain both about the surveillance and the lack of specific guidelines as the death certainly seemed awful to Stephen Handel.

"Did you notice the duration and level of pain of the mortal at the soccer match?"

"Yes, sir."

"And?"

"It lasted about twenty five minutes." It lasted forever.

"Precisely twenty six minutes seventeen seconds. The *duration* is critical. If you want to survive, you will have to conduct an unmistakably Excruciating Death! Do you understand?"

"Yes, sir."

When Ayodele spirited away Cornelius walked downtown, heading west on 52nd Street to Market Avenue, numbed by the reprimand. He wanted out of The Society of Death. Enough, he wondered, to suffer Expulsion? The menacing clatter of the El train shook Cornelius down to his skeletal underpinnings. He walked past a shuttered factory when two children approached on bicycles.

"What do you say, Padre? Bless us!"

Cornelius had forgotten to restore invisibility.

"Nice hoodie you've got!"

"Whatever," Cornelius grumbled, unsure if he had used the expression properly. He was relieved when the kids rode away.

8

Nineteen reapers of varying ranks were invited to watch *The Happening* in an inaccessible grotto at the Carlsbad Caverns; a row of scythes standing against a flowstone resembled a stack of weapons in a medieval armory. Rankled by the etiquette of the social gathering, Cornelius dodged conversation by pretending to examine the undulations of a rock wall with the intensity of a geologist.

Most of the invitees were strangers to Cornelius. He recoiled at the sight of gruesome 1st Tier Elijah, a victim of smallpox with a face of pustules and blisters. Another recognizable reaper, Wilkinson, moved with a military bearing. He had no right arm, lost to an improvised explosive device in Iraq, and advanced quickly to 2nd Tier because of the way he handled assignments regarding military veterans. Cornelius avoided Oliver, standing under an array of hollow mineral tubes hanging from the ceiling, who conducted reapings exclusively by tragic accident. Last Saturday in Kentucky he gathered the eight souls of a wedding party on the way to a sunset reception, including the bride and groom, by impairing the limousine driver as he drove over a small unlit bridge. The limo smashed through a rotted wood guardrail, careened down an embankment, and rolled over, immersing the long white vehicle and drowning the party.

Cornelius approached Houdon. He worked at the Queuing Station situated under Paris. Tasked with organizing the multitude of souls waiting to be replanted—especially important during wars and epidemics—he compared the job to herding sheep. Cornelius met Houdon at a symposium on the problems associated with the expanding mortal population, and learned that he was a serf of medieval France. Houdon was stocky with a stern face, and had lost a finger at some long-forgotten tavern when he reached for a scrap of roasted pig and another patron simultaneously stabbed at the collective dish. He looked sinister in the glow of the candles burning in the cavern.

"Bonjour, Cornelius. How are you?"

"Okay, always busy as a cadet. And you?"

"We're overworked at the Queuing Station from the SMRs of the North Korean Rice Revolution."

"We were always busy at the RD after a conflict, too." Cornelius brushed away a spider web. "Do you mind if I ask you a question?"

"Please."

"I'm curious about farming back when you were..."

"Mortal?" They moved past a stalagmite and waved to Kenny Danielson of the Entertainment Division, established to ease the widespread depression among reapers. "I tell you Corn, city dwellers imagine farming as idyllic. It was plain hard work. They've got machines nowadays, but it's still backbreaking."

Cornelius reminisced about his sixteen acre farm; he missed waking up each morning to milk Queen Anne. "I wish I was still a farmer."

"Keep your voice down. Do you want to get expelled?" Houdon pulled Cornelius back a few steps. "Anyway, I don't miss it. I was a plowman and tilled the soil."

"Were there problems on your farm?"

"Les Problèmes, oui!" Houdon picked up a candle, frowned at its scent and blew it out. As Houdon spoke of cruel landlords and peasant revolts, Cornelius noticed the haughty Roger Mortimer.

"We were always at war. Sometimes, we destroyed our crops to starve the enemy...sometimes our own country-man plundered our stores."

"Good evening, my young colleagues," shouted Ayodele, standing on top of a flat rock. "I am pleased to have you here at the Carlsbad Cavern Theatre." He encouraged the attendees to sit, Houdon and Cornelius found seats in back, away from the stage.

"Tonight we have a Hollywood classic," said Ayodele as the cavern quieted. "*The Happening* is a movie by my favorite director, M. Night Shyamalan, whom incidentally, I hope to reap one day."

A reaper went around the cave extinguishing the candles with a snuffer, leaving some on the rock stage for illumination.

"First," said Ayodele, "we have an alternative form of entertainment…a comedian." He introduced Danielson and receded to a dark recess of the cavern.

"Hey, reapers!" Danielson jumped up on the rock. "How the hell are you? Welcome to opening night, probably closing night, too." He mimed holding a microphone and pulling an imaginary wire.

"What's going on?" The crowd murmured. "Will someone tell me why do cloaks have to be dark? Damn monochromatic! Am I right? How about orange? Maybe green? I know, how about blood red?" He moved to the edge of the rock and pointed to Kao. "Have you ever considered smiling?"

Kao eyed Danielson with obvious contempt.

"Hey, I'm kidding," he said. "Put away your scythe!"

Cornelius surveyed the audience. He noticed Ayodele and Mortimer had vanished, probably to allow the gathered reapers to relax, and recognized 2nd Tiers Alfie and Frederik setting up a 35mm projector.

"Any Blue Oyster Cult fans here? Come on baby, watch out…don't fear the reaper, we'll be able to fly," sang Danielson, off-key. The crowd moaned. He tapped the imaginary microphone and made a piercing sound resembling audio feedback. "Hey, what about Jack the Reaper?

Man, he sure was fanatical about women…By the way, why are there no female reapers? I mean, seriously, women are naturally grim, certainly the ones I dated!" The issue of female reapers was controversial. Provocateurs favored expanding the roll of GRs by breaking with tradition and recruiting women, whereas the Traditionalists believed women lacked the instincts to reap. Danielson kept up the act as Frederik escorted him to the back of the cavern. "*Grim* Reaper. Why grim? I mean, who wants to be grim? How about the jolly reaper…the happy reaper? I know… the gay reaper…the scrolls would still read GR!"

2nd Tier Alfie drifted to the stage and presented a brief overview of *The Happening*, explaining how it explored the theme of Systematic Multiple Reapings. "A mysterious contagion threatens mortalkind and thousands commit suicide." He moved to the projector and brought the movie to life on a flat wall. "Now…The Happening."

9

Ayodele dominated death for sixteen centuries. He became a Grim Reaper in the winter of 419 while asleep and dreaming of flying with a flock of starlings. It was an uncomplicated time and the work of reapers was straightforward. The population of the planet stood at approximately one hundred million, and most mortals lived inconsequential lives as subsistence farmers or slaves, with no impact on The Divine Trajectory of Life. No distinction existed between the Easy and the Excruciating styles of death, and the world had yet to be organized into areas of responsibility (later, Ayodele created the model, dividing Africa, creating the Mediterranean Coastal and Sub-Saharan Zones, and separating Eurasia along the Ural Mountains to form the European and Asian Zones).

Ayodele was an elderly man when recruited, and once liberated from arthritis and gout, spirited around the globe with zeal, amazed by the agility and unlimited energy he possessed. He received no formal guidance—no cadet program yet existed—and struggled against the desire to exact revenge on lifelong rivals. Yet, as he completed assignments around the coast of the Mediterranean, he discovered that he excelled at death.

As a merchant of Ethiopia, Ayodele had profited from lucrative trade with Rome. As a reaper, he reveled in the ability to spirit around the imperial city. He was enraptured by its grandeur, and whenever possible visited the great temples, marveled at the architectural wonders, and attended debates in the senate. However, by 421, weakened by corruption and the repeated attacks of barbarians, Rome was vulnerable. Ayodele seized the opportunity.

One night, at the courtyard of the emperor, Ayodele observed the ambitious Constantius III organizing a military expedition to reunify the splintered empire. The emperor worked under an ornate lamp, and prayed to Bacchus—the god of wine—for the wisdom to restore the glory of Rome. Ayodele emerged from the dark wearing a patrician robe.

"Gallipor?" Constantius ate a fig. "Is that you?" The emperor barely glanced at Ayodele, lifted a wine goblet and turned to face the map on the wall. "If you are my new slave, you must learn how to approach your master properly."

The insolence enraged Ayodele, but he retained control. "Pardon, your glory, I am a new ambassador."

The irregular circumstance of such a visit caused Constantius to hesitate. "Ambassador?" The emperor slowly turned, put down the goblet and eyed a dagger. "If you are an ambassador, why have you come without ceremony? No, you are a low creature...an assassin...ambassador from hell!"

Ayodele bowed, conceding the point. He respected Constantius III and wanted to discuss the politics of the empire, but the poisoned wine was swift. The reaping of the brilliant and ambitious emperor hastened the fall of Rome. During the next several hundred years, as The Society of Death flourished, Ayodele grew in stature and prestige, and earned a reputation as a formidable Grim Reaper.

While on assignment in China during the 8th century, Ayodele learned the value of patience. As he conducted reconnaissance, Ayodele came to admire General An Lushan, a powerful military leader of the Tang Dynasty. When the ruthless general led a rebellion and established the rival Yan Dynasty, Ayodele exploited the crisis by perpetuating the civil war with reapings of key figures on both sides. By the time the revolt was crushed, the An Lushan Rebellion yielded 13,742,339 souls.

It was a celebrated achievement. Ayodele was rewarded with authorization to visit Africa; no formal Vacation of a Lifetime or Allowance to Act Mortal yet existed, purely an understanding of the importance of "sabbaticals." He spirited over marshes and grasslands, admired parades of elephants and giraffes. He spirited to the peak of Mount

Kilimanjaro, floated over the Mosi-ao-Tunya Falls on sheets of fresh water. Ayodele settled among a nomadic tribe west of Libya to rest, and lived as a mysterious hunter, reliably providing the tribe with game.

When Ayodele returned to China he spent hundreds of years conducting thousands of reapings. He was set to go to India, when he became intrigued by a band of Mongolian herders. While collecting intelligence about the clan, he observed the shaman prophesize that one boy in the village would grow to possess an ungodly desire to conquer foreign lands. Ayodele decided to protect the boy after he observed him kill his older brother during a hunt as they argued over the division of a carcass.

Whenever the destiny of the boy was threatened, Ayodele intervened, allowing the prophecy to be fulfilled: the boy became Genghis Khan.

Ayodele saved Khan in battles across Eurasia, and together, they caused the death of 11.09% of world population or 40,000,000 souls. By 1227, when he reaped Khan, Ayodele had earned the exclusive title of Master.

At present, Ayodele spirited over the dark circles of cinder in the Aïr Mountains of the Sahara Desert seeking the rare Barbary sheep. He spotted a herd of the agile goat-antelope and materialized, causing one to leap and the rest to scamper a few yards away. He adored the sandy-brown creatures and smiled at the old ones, which darken with age, and thought it would be peaceful to perish among the herd.

Ayodele accepted the inevitability of Termination. Most believed that when a Grim Reaper reached 1,607 years he devolved into a fundamental particle, imperishable, enduring as twilight—an instrumental part of the universe. Although it was blasphemous, he was tired of death. The world had changed. As an ever increasing number of mortals made unique contributions to the world, it necessitated more rules and regulations to prevent disrupting The Divine Trajectory of Life. As Master, he had the responsibility of upholding the new standards.

He also faced an unexpected challenge.

Normally reapers had 20/8 vision, but around the age of 1,500 years, Ayodele experienced diminished eyesight and struggled while spiriting over deserts and oceans. The impairments reminded Ayodele of how he had functioned before recruitment, when as a village elder he walked with a stick, led by a child guide. Recently he got lost along the Skeleton Coast in heavy fog and collided against a sand dune in the Namib Desert. The accident made Termination tangible. There were no records of weakened Grim Reapers, but Ayodele suspected such humiliating symptoms went unreported, no one would admit to such degradation.

Although he accepted that Termination was coming, Ayodele craved acknowledgement of how he had impacted the world. He was buoyed by suggestions made by 2nd

Tier Luboslaw to change the name of the Dwelling to The Ayodele or to change the designation of 1st Tier to Ayodele Tier, but these were modest legacies. He wanted to perform one last memorable act, something transformative.

10

"Sorry, termites," said Bill, pulling the rotted post of the clothesline out of the ground. "Tough to lose a good meal, huh?"

At least the worms will have a good meal, thought Cornelius. He decided to toughen up, adopt the attitude of Lewis Giles, a tanner by trade, and de facto sheriff of Natick back in the earliest days of the town. Giles held the view that protecting the welfare of the community "sometimes required gettin' dirty." Cornelius remembered his mother charitably comparing Giles to the disciple Peter, saying he was the "rock" of the praying village. Whenever a conflict arose among the inhabitants, Giles approached the parties involved holding the long, intimidating vat hook he used to dip the leather, and without fail, settled the issue. He put a stop to a range of bad behaviors, including fisticuffs and petty land disputes, thereby allowing the leaders to deliberate on theocratic issues and uphold a solemnity required to impart Christian standards. As Cornelius watched Bill lean the rotted post against the shed, he summoned the memory of Lewis Giles. The job of Grim Reaper sometimes required gettin' dirty.

The post fell to the ground. "Goddamn, Maria will have a fit." It was Wednesday—whites, and underwear, socks, and towels were dirtied. Leaning back, Bill pulled the line taut, and using an old broom handle as a temporary post, tied the line so it hung off the ground. Bill phoned Maria to say he was going to the hardware store, and Cornelius spirited to the car.

The car backfired. Bill went to the house for two antacids. He tried it again. "What was it Mims use to say?" Bill smiled. "Patience is a virtue, have it if you can...always in a woman, seldom in a man." He cheered when the engine turned over, and drove down the boulevard and made a left onto Ashbury Avenue.

Cornelius read the scroll carefully. Sixty eight year-old Bill White of Neptune Township, New Jersey, had struggled financially for years, but hoped to pay for a small wedding for his daughter Stephanie. He maneuvered the car past the potholes and complained about the frost heaves. The hardware store always sold cheap, odd pieces of wood, and he planned to replace the pole and rewash the clothes before Maria got home.

A stab of indigestion turned to severe pain. Bill managed to guide the car to the shoulder of the road and turned on the hazard lights. He retrieved aspirin tablets from the bottom of a pocket. Cornelius moved to complete the reaping. Bill dropped the pills, and searched under his crotch and on the dirty floor mat, but Cornelius had flicked each pill under the brake pedal. Seventeen seconds. Bill gasped for breath, squeezing the shirt tight as if to wring it dry. "Please God," he moaned. "I want to be a Grandpa. Plea..."

Bill collapsed forward and knocked the gear shift lever into neutral, causing the car to roll backwards, downhill toward oncoming traffic. Cornelius grimaced, and ignoring the Code of Conduct, shifted the car back into park. He was no Lewis Giles.

The temperature in the region surrounding the Dwelling was a bitter 3° Fahrenheit. Despite the weather tourists kept flying from Oslo to the nearby town of Longyearbyen, and cruise liners continued to travel past the skerry as the shipping lanes were warmed by the waters of the West Svalbard Current. Cornelius was aware of the activity, but detached, set apart. Isolated.

Cornelius was filled with angst. Although he had no desire for assignments, he felt it was a bad omen that he had none when the rest of the cadets were busy. Tristan was in Texas at the Dallas Cowboys practice facility to reap a linebacker, Levi went to Santa Fe to assist an arsonist and facilitate a Systematic Multiple Reaping, and Javier was at the office of a Denver plastic surgeon to cause fatal complications during the rhinoplasty of a sixteen year-old girl.

A heavy, wet snow fell. Cornelius made a snowball and tossed it at an outcropping of rock on the skerry, it remained clean despite a dozen attempts to hit it. He wondered about the distribution of assignments. They were supposedly kept fair and balanced by using an arcane formula. Linnaeus had worked it over and, unable to detect a pattern, and concluded no blueprint existed, that assignments were likely distributed "by the very mortal inclinations of opportunism and favoritism."

Grim Reapers received assignments at precisely 12:00:00 Central European Time; no mortal ever died by the touch of a reaper at that moment. While reapers were dormant, markings emerged on their forearms with the name, gender, age and type of death for each assignment. A biographical scroll of each individual simultaneously appeared in The Book of Expiration Dates, the book was roughly sixty seven thousand pages and mysteriously changed to reflect every death, every day.

Cornelius walked around the Dwelling, brooding over a recent Event conducted by Levi. The former insurance salesman showed no scruples when he exploited a crisis at a Nebraskan prison in which inmates held several security guards hostage. While an expert negotiator calmed the leader of the prisoners and the stand-off moved toward a resolution, Levi pulled up the rifle of an officer on the SWAT team and squeezed the trigger. The random gunshot panicked the inmates, causing the deaths of one officer and nine prisoners. Ayodele called it an "exceptional accomplishment" and challenged the rest of the cadets to be equally exceptional.

Cornelius sat down to carve the tusk when he heard a group of snowmobilers motor up and down a valley on neighboring Bear Island, the original home of the Dwelling. Established in 1601, the dorm accommodated five cadets, replacing the old practice of lodging cadets with 3rd Tiers. Bear Island remained secluded until the 20th century, when mortals began traipsing across the Svalbard archipelago and threatening its isolation. When two cadets overreacted to the proximity of a dirigible and crashed the airship *Italia* as it passed overhead, the Dwelling was "temporarily" moved to its current home on the skerry; officially, relocating to a new, permanent locale remained under consideration.

Cornelius put away the tusk when Tristan materialized, banging a stick on the ice, a plodding tempo evocative of Taps. Cornelius deemed it a hostile gesture, but an unspoken détente formed when a boat passed with two crew-members pointing binoculars at the skerry.

"The waters around here are damn busy," Tristan griped.

Cornelius put away the tusk, climbed up a pile of rocks and thought he spotted polar bears on Bear Island—disappointed to find it was only men wearing white parkas.

"What is it?" Tristan asked.

"Just a couple of people, I mean mortals." Cornelius remained guarded around Tristan, but the tension between them had seemed to ease.

"You know," said Tristan, chewing on a pinch of snow as if it was tobacco, "the Dwelling should have more style."

"We're cadets, what do you expect?"

"What about moving it to Las Vegas? Maybe the penthouse of a hotel, I know, how about a bank vault with loads of cash?"

"We hardly ever used cash when I was alive."

"I don't know, things aren't fair," said Tristan, shaking his head.

"What do you mean?"

"Look at you, stuck here without any assignments."

"I get lots of assignments."

"Yeah, sure, you get little old ladies, broken down men, and pathetic slobs, but no interesting ones, no celebrities or politicians."

"Get lost." Cornelius walked away, watching the bearded men across the strait extract long tubes of ice from the tundra. He turned when he heard a splash. It was Tristan holding the stick, now dripping with saltwater. A weapon. He jabbed Cornelius. It burned a hole through the cloak and melted his skin, exposing the head of his left humeral bone. Cornelius clutched his shoulder, stunned by the pain. "Damn you! I swear..."

"Yeah?" Tristan waved the stick. "You'll do what?" He flicked droplets of saltwater at Cornelius, burning tiny holes in his cloak as if it was hit with buckshot.

The scientists were gone, so Cornelius escaped to Bear Island. A drop of saltwater on the edge of the cloak slid down to his left Achilles tendon, causing searing pain and exposing the fibrous tissue. He wanted to kill Tristan. He moved to the spot on the island where the men had drawn ice samples, and if Tristan pursued, Cornelius planned to use the holes—filled with saltwater—as a trap.

The pain was short-lived, but Cornelius was edgy, unsettled by the attack and unsure of what to do. He moved to the campsite of the scientists and listened outside their tent:

"I say we rise at dawn, and investigate the properties of the snow beyond the archipelago."

"Agreed. I pray the Spectral Radiation Buoys work as advertised."

Cornelius peeked through the ventilation holes and saw the two men wrapped tight inside sleeping bags. Their conversation left him bewildered, and when they turned out the hi-tech electric lantern he returned to the skerry. Tristan was gone so he entered a chamber, and protected by its mysterious properties, stood dormant.

After a fitful dormancy, Cornelius awakened to assignments on both forearms. Two on the left were female, and two on the right were male. Out of curiosity, he rubbed the markings, but they were as permanent as a tattoo, only vanishing upon completion of the task. He put on the damaged cloak, draping it to conceal both the holes in the fabric and the exposed tendons and bone of his left shoulder and ankle, and reviewed the scrolls.

The Book of Expiration Dates indicated Norah Al-Kazaz was scheduled to die at 9:19 a.m. Eastern Standard Time. He skimmed over the scroll; Norah was a nineteen year-old sophomore at William & Mary, majoring in philosophy, with plans to attend law school. The young woman was to die an Easy Death.

Held up by a hailstorm over the Chesapeake Bay, Cornelius arrived with only eighteen minutes to plan and organize an Event. He searched the campus and spotted Norah jogging down Duke of Gloucester Street and listening to Morcheeba on her iPod. A sports car sped down Route 5 and turned up Duke of Gloucester Street, the driver reduced speed when he saw Norah. Frantic, Cornelius penetrated the car and knocked over a cup, spilling scalding coffee across the right thigh of the driver, causing him to extend the leg and unintentionally accelerate. Cornelius used the scythe to turn the steering wheel and the Audi R8 hit Norah, catching her body under the car and dragging it down the street, spewing blood across the forsythias planted along the road.

The driver wailed uncontrollably. A few people came over to the accident; a woman called 9-1-1, an elderly man placed his jacket over Norah. Sirens filled the street. EMTs and police arrived. From the roof of a parked SUV, Cornelius watched the majestic chiffon soul of Norah depart the body. Despondent, he turned away and spirited to Bermuda.

Although the British Overseas Territory was farther from the North American coast than Cornelius expected, he still had enough time to visit the Bermuda National Library at Par-la-Ville in Hamilton. He promised Linnaeus he would "read, read, read" whenever he got a chance, and the library might help him to stop obsessing over the gruesome death of Norah. He stole clothes from an unattended rack on the sidewalk in front of a swanky shop—another commandment broken, he thought—and moved to the library. He materialized in a desolate row filled with books on tax codes. He stored the scythe on a shelf, and walked out to the main circulation area wearing a pair of sandals, a polo shirt, and long slacks that covered the hole in his Achilles tendon.

The library was painted a soft tropical yellow and filled with vases of fragrant begonias and orchids. Cornelius picked up a brochure on the local Natural History Museum, fascinated to learn about its collection of sea shells. Then he got an easy-to-read book about the region and sat on a windowsill, admiring the pictures of the island. He smiled at the characterization of the Bermuda Triangle as only a myth, knowing the Bermudian Tricorne—as designated by the original GR of the region—was real. He wanted to stay and read, but he had rushed the assignment on Norah, and the next assignment required preparation.

Latanya Gabaldon, a divorced investment banker, had sole custody of twin eight year-old daughters—Bertrise, studious and mathematical, and Molly, impulsive and creative. They lived in a condominium at Hidden Cove. Cornelius stalked the family as they loaded a Land Rover and confirmed the license plate number. As the biographical sketch indicated, the girls had curly brown hair like their mother.

They arrived at a secluded beach and the girls spread out a blanket and dumped out a bag filled with pails and shovels. Latanya opened a beach chair. Cornelius adored the pink sand and the cirrus clouds gliding leisurely across the horizon. He longed to touch the turquoise water, and as Latanya slathered the girls with sunscreen, he played stowaway on a nearby sailboat. Two men maneuvered it away from the dock. Cornelius settled atop the mast as the boat rocked gently, fascinated by the wet-suits of the men and watched as they each pulled on fins, put on oxygen tanks, and pulled down eye masks. It reminded him of harnessing a team of horses.

Approximately a hundred yards away he heard a splash, and he spirited out to discover a pair of dolphins, absolutely amazed by the graceful creatures. Back at the sailboat the couple kissed, held hands and tipped backward, submerging under the water—a sad reminder of Skowron, but they reemerged, swimming playfully with the dolphins.

Cornelius returned to the beach. Latanya was eating a banana while the girls gobbled watermelon slices. He was unwilling to destroy a family, but wondered if one memorable Event would satisfy Ayodele and Páll, at least for awhile. He had the wild idea of finding a brown recluse spider and using the pain of its bite to cause a fatal incident, but rejected it as impractical. Frustrated, he considered violating the terms of the assignment by turning the Easy Death into an Excruciating one, but he was revulsed by the prospect.

As the girls played in the soft waves at the shore, a shadow crept across the beach. It was Ayodele, hovering over a dune and racing over to Latanya. Cornelius witnessed the Master point and the woman droop.

"What happened?" Ayodele asked sharply. "Where were you?"

"I don't know, I was..."

"The mortal was scheduled at 10:03!"

"But Master...I had almost an hour."

Ayodele turned and walked away.

Cornelius watched, struck by the lack of footprints on the sand, and realized Bermuda was in the Atlantic/Bermuda Time Zone, one hour ahead of Virginia. "Um, Master...I'm sorry...The time zone...I...I..."

Alarmed by the distant shrieks of the girls, Cornelius scurried down the beach to catch up to Ayodele.

The Master came to a stop, and used a piece of driftwood to write on the beach as artfully as a calligrapher in a language unfamiliar to Cornelius. "Have you ever heard of Kitum Cave?" he asked.

"No, Master." Cornelius feared the cave functioned as a stockade. The words on the sand vanished under a gentle wave.

"Elephants frequent the long tunnel of Kitum to lick salt off the walls and gain sustenance."

A cave of salt! The vision horrified Cornelius.

"What am I to do with you?" Ayodele almost sounded compassionate. "The assignment you completed in Virginia led to unscheduled deaths."

The accusation hit Cornelius hard. He went over the assignment. Norah Al-Kazaz was reaped on schedule, without a problem. It was, as Páll would say, "clean."

"Were you late arriving to Virginia?"

Cornelius learned growing up to always tell the truth. Natick of the 17th century was tight-knit, populated almost exclusively with extended families, and everyone knew what everybody else was up to, there was no way to *not* to tell the truth. Still, he equivocated. "I arrived on schedule." The penetrating gaze of Ayodele made Cornelius clarify. "I left myself inadequate time to prepare."

"Exactly," stated Ayodele. "If you had, you would have read in the scroll that Norah was a foreign exchange student from Saudi Arabia. The manner of her death led to the unscheduled deaths of three mortals, trampled during a protest in Egypt over the killing of an Arab woman by an American."

Cornelius stared out at the Atlantic Ocean. He was guilty of unscheduled deaths—again. Not on the scale of the Great Fire of London, but that was no consolation, and now he had botched the assignment in Bermuda.

"You were fortunate the mortals were of no consequence to The Divine Trajectory of Life." Ayodele faced Cornelius. "Now, I ask you, do you *want* to be a Grim Reaper Cadet? If not, I will place you at the Queuing Station, or back at the RD. I grant you this one opportunity to change your status."

It was a chance to get away. Cornelius considered that maybe the RD with Linnaeus was the right job—tedious, but a secure position with no risks. But, what if the suggestion by Ayodele was bait? Unsure what to do, and with the sand sliding away and the waves reaching out to grab hold, he impulsively, almost involuntarily, blurted, "I want to be a cadet!"

Ayodele arched an eyebrow. "As you wish, but I warn you, raise your standards...or you will suffer." He ascended to the sky and vanished. Dazed, Cornelius returned to the docks. He removed the half-carved walrus tusk from the secret pocket of his cloak and dropped it in the water.

Cornelius rode a southwesterly air current to Florida and descended at the Jacksonville Zoo & Gardens—double-checked the time—and settled over the Plains of the East Africa exhibit.

He loved to be among the Nile crocodiles and the Eastern bongos and pink-backed pelicans, comforted by the fact reapers had no power over nature and were unable to hurt the animals. He watched two enormous rhinos walk to the lake for a drink, and using the power of a reaper, landed on the back of one. The animal shifted its body and moved its ears. Cornelius stroked its rough hide and the rhino wagged its tail. A few acres away he approached a lion resting under the shade of a tree and jumped when it roared, astounded by its ferocity. He wanted to explore the rest of the savanna, but he intended to handle the next job properly and sought out Nicholas Leavitt.

The scroll indicated that the seventy one year-old man worked full-time as the conductor of the train at the Jacksonville Zoo and Gardens. The attraction was popular with families; small children loved the smooth ride and the ice cream available in the restored 19th century station. Cornelius sat atop the caboose as Nicholas brought the train to a stop and handed out plastic train whistles to the small children as they disembarked.

There were several minutes before the next scheduled ride, and Nicholas went to the shed for a screwdriver to fix the rattling side panel of a passenger car. He unlocked the shed and stepped in, but the door swung shut. He cursed the wind and pulled out a pocket flashlight. "Holy crap, what are you doing in here?"

"I was, um..." Cornelius had expected it to remain dark. "I was looking for a bathroom."

"This isn't an outhouse, kid," said Nicholas. "The station has facilities." He moved the flashlight up and down, squinting at Cornelius. "You hiding any of my tools under that...whatever you're wearing?"

It was time. Cornelius administered a massive heart attack, relieved it was at least out of sight of the families waiting at the train station. He decided in the future to do whatever was necessary to avoid any interaction with the "assignment."

Cornelius wafted over the Everglades, reveling in the sawgrass prairie and the cypresses and ponds. A thunderstorm gathered and released a lighting strike, igniting a fire and destroying a few acres of grass. When it subsided he inspected the damage, the roots of the blackened scrub had survived. He smiled when he saw a turtle emerge unharmed.

The storm moved east. He drifted with a tropical breeze over the vast prairie; the wide open space nourished Cornelius. As he sailed over the brackish water he came to rest on a red mangrove tree. The peace of the Everglades allowed Cornelius to sort out muddled thoughts he had about the day he died.

He remembered moving around an English hamlet with Páll, aware he was dead. Strangely, it poured rain but they stayed dry, while the villagers got soaked. The experience had the strange reality of a vibrant dream. Páll explained that Cornelius was "transformed" and just as farmers harvest crops, Grim Reapers harvest souls. They were a special part of the universe, selected by a mystical power to contribute to the lifecycle, and lived an incredible existence of over fifteen hundred years, long enough to experience the future. A divine gift, claimed Páll.

Resting atop the mangrove tree, Cornelius wished he could return the "gift."

The tender movement of the tidal estuary bordering the mangrove mesmerized Cornelius. The sun glare sparkled brilliantly. He glided out over the sea, and imagined a mermaid soaking up the sun and singing a sad song.

11

The Provocateurs were a decentralized movement, and, as a result, lacked coherence. Some argued publicly at conferences, confident that logic would lead to change. This was demonstrated by 3rd Tier Charles Tallow at the Cliffs of Pico Bolivar when he successfully argued for the adoption of the mortals' system for measuring time.

Provocateurs rarely challenged the old ways head-on. Once a 3rd Tier unwisely attempted to warn a mortal of impending death, and was sentenced to Expulsion in the Dead Sea (the high salt concentration and buoyancy made it an extraordinarily long-drawn-out death). The ill-advised plan had the unintended consequence of leading to the establishment of an investigative unit called the Policiá, which seemed to help the Traditionalists maintain the status quo. The most dramatic attempt to revolutionize what the Provocateurs considered "sclerotic customs" was a secretive plan led by 2nd Tier Luboslaw.

Luboslaw devised a stratagem to surreptitiously recruit a female Grim Reaper Cadet. The practice of strictly male reapers was so sacrosanct that nobody ever felt the need to confirm the gender of a new recruit. The long-term goal of the plan by Luboslaw aimed to balance reaperkind with female GRs, and thereby reduce the disproportionate number of Excruciating Deaths applied to women.

In discussions with trusted confidants, Luboslaw outlined the parameters of the ideal candidate: strong-willed enough to both reap souls as assigned—whenever and wherever, without hesitation, probably for decades—and one, who as a mortal, demonstrated self-sufficiency and resilience. A rare mix of qualities. The woman would build an unchallenged record of success as a cadet, and when the Provocateurs revealed her true identity, the absurdity of the discrimination against females would be self-evident.

Forty two years ago he found the right woman.

Luboslaw explained the workings of The Society of Death to the dying woman, as rapid as an impulse across a synapse, and conveyed how a female Grim Reaper had the opportunity to help mortal women around the world. He emphasized that the scheme was a gamble, the odds of success long, and failure meant a painful execution. Nevertheless, the woman accepted the role.

Over the decades, Luboslaw witnessed the courage of the young woman. The cadet demonstrated exceptional intelligence and skill, and the plan unfolded without a problem; only once did the agent almost falter, it happened at the 1976 Summer Olympics in Montréal when she was assigned to reap a boxer and at the appointed time he was taking a shower.

Now, as spirited up and down the streets of Gdansk, Luboslaw was troubled. He had received instructions from the lone 1st Tier Provocateur that the woman must recruit another cadet, one "viscerally" motivated to disrupt the machinations of Roger Mortimer. Luboslaw protested that the deviation from the original mission put the woman at greater risk, but he relented when the 1st Tier explained the very survival of the Provocateurs was at stake.

12

The next assignment scared Cornelius. It mandated another Excruciating Death, and after the admonishment from Ayodele over the inadequate death of Stephen Handel, he knew he had better get it right. Páll ordered that he travel by bus, a decidedly sluggish mode of transportation to allow Cornelius time to consider the consequences of failure: inflict a genuinely Excruciating Death or suffer a torturous Expulsion.

The bus ride was unbearable. Encaged by the bus seat, he looked out the window, disappointed by the countryside—as dull as the skerry—buildings, parking lots, littered roadsides, repeating over and over, mile after mile. The stultifying interior of the bus made it impossible to relax, with overhead televisions playing a movie about a talking dog and a detective, and the buzz of neighboring headphones disturbingly similar to the sound made by reapers when they materialize. Cornelius wanted to spirit out the emergency escape. He recalled that as a boy when bored at church he would pose as if praying and imagine an adventure. He shut his eyes and imagined riding

Arabella to Boston to pick up a satchel of letters, but it was no use. He was pestered by memories of the Replanting Department.

The work of the RD was tiresome. Cornelius thought it was better suited to a librarian or an accountant, not an ex-farmer. Sitting on the bus, he recalled the unpleasant negotiations he conducted with the Great Spirit of the Gulper Eel. He initiated the exchange with the customary reverential statement: "Great Spirit of the Gulper Eel! I request the honor of an audience."

"Yebbb," responded the Great Spirit. Cornelius struggled to ignore the oozing fluids flowing out of the over-sized mouth of the Great Spirit as it pierced the surface of the Indian Ocean, lured by the promise of additional souls. It responded with the time-honored code, dripping, "Persuadebbe!"

"As a mortal, this soul had a giant mouth," explained Cornelius, endeavoring to persuade. "He lived as a politician, a vainglorious and malicious liar. We at the RD believe placement as a Gulper Eel, living consciously at the bottom of the ocean, will teach the Deputy Minister lessons he needs in order to evolve."

"Veryebbe Wellebbe," agreed the Great Spirit of the Gulper Eel, accepting the soul to complete the transaction.

The bus traveled north on I-95 and exited at Dillon, South Carolina and came to a rest stop. Cornelius eagerly stepped off, and following protocol to "conform to the norms", got on line at the Bojangles' Famous Chicken n' Biscuits and ordered a country ham biscuit and a bottle of water. He walked a short distance away from the bus and pretended to consume the meal; the odor was awful.

He got back on the bus, took a swig of water and resumed the appearance of napping. As the passengers straggled back, Cornelius recalled the last placement he negotiated at the RD. It involved the Great Spirit of the Warthog residing in southern Africa.

"Great Spirit of the Warthog! I request the honor of an audience."

"Welcome!" responded the Great Spirit of the Warthog; its voice, when translated, retained minimal grunts and slurps.

"When mortal, Tiffany lived as a wealthy hotelier, a woman of privilege, who lacked the higher qualities of the soul."

The Great Spirit chortled. "You expect a whore to have higher qualities?"

"Please pardon the inaccurate translation, Great Spirit...*hotelier*."

"Hotelier, yes, I understand."

"The Replanting Department believes Tiffany will derive value as a self-aware warthog forever rutting, with a bald head filled with warts and covered with insects."

"What advantage do *we* gain?" inquired the Great Spirit of the Warthog. There were no charitable replantings.

"As a female warthog, Tiffany will contribute to the expansion of your population." Cornelius gestured in the direction of several male warthogs.

The Great Spirit of the Warthog articulated a detailed cost-benefit analysis, before granting the request. Cornelius recorded the task as complete when the soul of Tiffany was transmuted to a female warthog and greeted by a pair of aroused males.

The bus sped down the highway. Cornelius was wretched, unable to sit still. He felt similarly trapped at cave of the RD, only saved by the camaraderie of Linnaeus. They shared a special bond—both were guilty of notorious transgressions that caused unscheduled deaths.

Linnaeus was aboard the maiden voyage of the Titanic to harvest Captain Edward J. Smith. While strolling around, admiring the ship, he found the well-stocked library and became transfixed about the flora and fauna of the Amazon rainforest. As a result he neglected to take the captain at the appointed time. If Smith had died on schedule it would have inevitably delayed the Titanic, enough to avoid the iceberg and prevent the unscheduled deaths of thousands.

Although reassignment to the RD was viewed as a downgrade, Linnaeus thrived. Its mission was to give each individual a chance to evolve, and to do so, a soul had to be placed in the appropriate organism—a task that allowed Linnaeus to be a scientist again as he researched the natural world to make optimal placements.

Enlightened mortals were replanted as highly developed animals, such as elephants, dolphins, pigs, crows, and chimpanzees. Most mortals were placed as lower life forms to learn a particular virtue. Reapers held no leverage over the natural world. Therefore in order to place a depraved mortal, the RD had to negotiate with the Great Spirit of a creature. Linnaeus was appointed Manager of the RD when he miraculously replanted the shriveled souls of Hitler, Stalin, and Mao, and promised the Great Spirit of the Dung Beetle exclusive rights to future dictators.

During periods of downtime at the RD, Linnaeus taught Cornelius how to play dominoes. Cornelius invariably lost actual games, but he loved to stack long rows and tip one and watch as they collapsed. A true guilty pleasure as the pursuit of joy was discouraged. He usually went to Copenhagen to stack dominoes up and down the staircases of an abandoned refrigeration factory. The dominoes were made of natural materials and visible to mortals, so vigilance was crucial. The factory was safe, but dull. One evening, Cornelius sought a new locale in Europe. He spotted an intriguing soccer stadium, vacant and dilapidated, superior to the refrigeration factory in every way, with nooks, corners, and great heights. He poured out the bag of dominoes that he had painstakingly carved, and strategically used cracks in the marble surface to form curling and winding rows. The moonlight created a row of silhouetted dominoes. It was the only time Cornelius heard Linnaeus shout:

"Why are you up here?" demanded Linnaeus, unexpectedly materializing, and swooping down to collect the dominoes. "You're on the Roman Colosseum!"

"What?" Cornelius turned at the sound of car horns from the street. Distracted, he knocked a domino over the edge, and watched with terror as someone on the street picked it up. If examined it would reveal how it came from the bones of the extinct Tahitian sandpiper, collected by Cornelius in 1773, but carved within the last year. It was a serious violation—losing a handmade object to a mortal potentially compromised The Society of Death.

"What do we do about the domino?" begged Cornelius as the mortal walked away.

"We do nothing," said Linnaeus. "We rely on the high probability that it will not cause a problem."

"We do *nothing*?"

"Yes, don't you see, an unauthorized reaping produces a greater risk of unforeseen consequences."

Cornelius yielded to the logic of Linnaeus, but as he remembered it now, riding on the foul-smelling bus to

Delaware, he obsessed over how one domino had the power to produce a chain reaction.

The bus arrived at New Castle Airport. Cornelius filed out with the passengers, relieved to get off the cramped vehicle. He went to a public restroom, dematerialized in a stall and spirited out a window.

Dr. Zwetchkenbaum—Dr. ZZ—was a fan of ZZ Top and sometimes wore a long costume beard during rounds at the hospital. He was a fifty four year-old widow with no children, and found purpose as a volunteer with Médecins Sans Frontières. Dr. ZZ had previously worked in Juba, South Sudan, as a general surgeon and he wanted to go back and help establish a modern hospital. He had no difficulty obtaining a leave of absence from Good Samaritan Regional Medical Center, and merely complained that the trip required another round of vaccinations.

As he waited at Concourse E, Gate 9 with several passengers watching a heavy sleet fall, Dr. ZZ told an attractive young woman about the mission. "A couple years ago, I worked with a remarkable group. It included professionals from five countries. There were many limitations and deprivations. I remember we sterilized equipment using an autoclave over a propane burner."

The grounds crew de-iced the wings of the Boeing 717. When it taxied to the terminal, the jet was slightly out of reach the passenger walkway so the crew maneuvered an adapter into position to act as a bridge. Cornelius saw an opportunity and spirited down to the runway. He scanned the nearby area, and imperceptibly rolled an aircraft jack forward, unnoticed in the inclement weather, and parked it directly under the walkway.

Dr. ZZ glanced out the window at the sleet, and then approached the man at the ticket counter. "Any delays tonight?"

"No, sir, we have clearance. Flight 49 to Kennedy is on schedule."

"Thank you."

"You're welcome, sir."

Cornelius took position on the console of the passenger walkway. It had a complicated computer screen and multiple buttons, and though he had no time to test the key element of the Event, he understood the purpose of the joystick.

They announced the flight and Dr. ZZ joined the line forming at the gate. He popped a chewable Dramamine, and grabbed the copy of *Lancet* he packed at the bottom of his carry-on bag. The doors opened and the line advanced down the walkway. Dr. ZZ shuffled forward, engrossed in an article about infection control and unaware that the walkway had jerked apart from the adapter, exposing a two-foot wide gap. He stepped over the edge, fell seven feet down and struck the handle of the aircraft jack, rupturing both testicles before hitting the tarmac.

He lay face down on an oil stain, shrieking with pain. A ground crew man knelt beside Dr. ZZ. "You're going to be all right...I called for an ambulance."

Another man arrived. "What happened?"

The grounds crew man pointed up to the gap—now filled with gawking faces—between the passenger walkway and the adapter.

Cornelius moved to the top of the plane and waited, and although pained by the groans of Dr. ZZ, he was terrified when he heard a siren.

The ambulance approached, but it skidded and hit a parked truck. It stalled while backing away, and a pair of paramedics got out and ran across the runway. Flustered, Cornelius moved to stop the EMTs from performing lifesaving heroics, but Dr. ZZ died—as scheduled in The Book of Expiration Dates. The grounds crew personnel looked away, one prayed out loud.

The guilt over the Excruciating Death of Dr. ZZ overwhelmed Cornelius—he felt he had committed an unforgiveable sin. He rushed back to the Dwelling, seeking the refuge of a dormant state.

Alerted by the sun, Cornelius practically fell out of the chamber. He put on his cloak, and checked both forearms, both were blank. There was no visit from Ayodele or Páll. Cornelius half-expected a rebuke because of the slapdash quality of the Excruciating Death of Dr. ZZ. He replayed the Event over compulsively, believing it was only the dumb luck of the ambulance skidding that made it work.

It was quiet at the Dwelling. Heavy fog reduced the traffic of the shipping lanes, and Tristan and Levi were out on assignments. Javier received a Vacation of a Lifetime for orchestrating multiple cases of SIDS in Los Angeles and chose to live as a policeman in Bogotá, Colombia. The city had one of the highest murder rates in the world and as its policeman Javier would have an ideal vantage point from which to enjoy the grisly crime scenes.

Depressed, Cornelius resisted the urge to return to the chamber. He was afraid he would be stay for decades and be labeled an apathetic reaper, relegated to inactive status and imprisoned on an abandoned oil rig in the Baltic Sea. There he would be deliberately dangled over saltwater as a warning to recover or face Expulsion. In the past, prevalent cases of apathy caused significant problems, an epidemic once led to a dramatic drop in reapings and lasted almost two hundred years; mortals referred to the era as the Pax Romana.

Cornelius walked over to an outcropping of rock with a protective ledge. He retrieved a branch of Lebanon cedar he had acquired on a trip to the RD and recalled the admonition from Linnaeus: "The Cedrus lebani is a rare tree. I hope you took a fallen or broken branch." Cornelius cleaned the knotted stick using a straight chisel he borrowed from a Home Depot in Philadelphia, and wondered if he were capable of carving a piccolo. The meditative work of carving pacified Cornelius. Life was simple, he thought, death complicated.

13

While conducting the Excruciating Death of French artist Théodore Géricault, Ayodele was inspired to paint. Although self-taught, he created a stunning portrait of Medhat holding a staff and ankh. Ayodele had it framed with antique scythe handles, and the painting now hung in the Cadet Workshop. In time it became the iconic image of the great Egyptian.

All cadets were commanded to attend tutorials at the workshop, housed in an undiscovered cavity of the Pyramid of Djoser. A course on Medhat was central to the curriculum. Presently, the fabled GR proved a divisive subject as both Traditionalists and Provocateurs evoked the icon to support their respective agendas. Traditionalists believed Medhat worked around the Euphrates and Tigris rivers as civilization developed, and pointed to the hieroglyphic symbol of the Amenta in the Pyramid of Djoser to substantiate the legend. They revered Medhat and perceived any change as sacrilege (zealots among the Traditionalists used a staff instead of a scythe). Provocateurs emphasized that Medhat was the representation of the true purpose of death—renewal to promote the life cycle. They viewed modifications, such as the Time Protocol, Vacation of a Lifetime and the Entertainment Division, as important adaptations to a rapidly changing world, and argued the real sacrilege was the abuse of power by some 1st Tiers.

Although agitated by the cramped conditions of the pyramid lit by two candles, Cornelius endured the rambling tutorial presented by Páll, grateful for the distraction from recurring visions of Dr. ZZ suffering on the airport tarmac.

Páll droned pedantically: "We reapers were portrayed by ancient scholars of the Bible as Abaddon the Destroyer, or as the Angel of the Abyss. Some mortal cultures honor the Grim Reaper as a woman!" Páll cackled—it reverberated, causing dust and dirt to seep out of crevices. "The cloak we wear and the scythe we hold are the style of the day. Medhat wore a loincloth and carried a staff. In some parts of the world, reapers wore white cloaks and wide hats, or used brooms, rakes, or swords."

Kao yawned, a peculiar remnant from life. It amused Cornelius, remembering how he got smacked as a boy whenever he yawned during a church service.

"Images from Europe during the period of the Black Plague show a reaper driving a cart to haul the corpses... we had no such responsibility." Páll moved over to a tomb, tracing its edge with a finger.

Kao raised a hand. "May I ask a question?"

"Of course."

"How do we validate that instructions actually originate from the Triumvirate?"

"That's a ridiculous question." Páll frowned. "You simply obey!"

Kao sat impassively. Cornelius was curious about the Triumvirate—Traditionalists speculated it consisted of three rival reapers, conquerors, poets, merchants, or ascetics, to balance reapings around the globe, in contrast, the Provocateurs viewed it as a myth. He wanted to ask, but hesitated to aggravate Páll.

"Let us proceed to reapings by gunfire. One of my favorites, administered by the esteemed 1st Tier Nathan Eackler, involved the death of Alexander Hamilton." Páll paced as he articulated the facts: A duel occurred on the morning of July 11th, 1804, in New Jersey at the Heights of Weehawken, between the Vice President of the United States Aaron Burr, and the retired Treasury Secretary Hamilton. The two antagonists had developed mutual resentments over the years, exacerbated by the publication of a letter, guided by 1st Tier Eackler to the *Albany Register* indicating Hamilton fervently believed Burr was, "a dangerous man…not to be trusted with the reins of government."

Páll smiled. "The coup de grâce came when 1st Tier Eackler made sure Burr aimed the pistol so the bullet struck Hamilton lethally."

Cornelius raised a hand to inquire about "coup de grâce" but Páll ignored him and lectured about the use of assassinations and random gun-fire. "Excellent, we have covered the topic of reapings by gunshot. Now, I want to acquaint you with reapings by inclement weather."

"We have no control over the natural world," asserted Kao.

"Obviously!" Páll held up an index finger as a warning. "Reapings by inclement weather *exploit* natural conditions to maximize death. You have much to learn, cadet!"

"Yes, sir," said Kao.

Páll proceeded to provide examples of how to use hurricanes, tornadoes, tsunamis, earthquakes or volcanic eruptions to expand a Systematic Multiple Reaping.

"At our next meeting, we will review basic anatomy so you may best exploit mortal frailties," said Páll. He bid farewell and abruptly spirited out of the pyramid, inadvertently extinguishing one candle.

"You're courageous to question Páll," said Cornelius.

"Somebody had to."

Cornelius sidestepped the subtle insult. "You've got a perfect record, I'm barely hanging on."

"I apologize." Kao smiled.

Cornelius pointed at the smile. "That's a code violation!"

"You ought to know."

"All right, all right," said Cornelius, holding up his hands as if surrendering. "Let's get out of here, please."

Kao suggested they head east together to Mount Fuji. Cornelius accepted the invitation, curious about the top-rated cadet.

Cornelius followed Kao around the peak of Mount Fuji, enchanted by its beautiful cone white with snow. The expansive vista helped shake the claustrophobia from the dim interior of the Egyptian pyramid with its daunting image of Medhat and the overbearing Páll. Kao pointed to a hollow in the side of the mountain. They sailed out of altocumulus clouds and landed softly at the edge of the private Dwelling. Cornelius peered down a corridor that led to a chamber. He saw no back wall, only shadows, but when he considered the neighbors he had on the skerry, it was a treasure.

"Thanks for inviting me up here."

Kao smiled. "I have something for you." He presented the half-carved walrus tusk that Cornelius had dropped in the water back in Bermuda. "I retrieved it with a hand net. I assumed you would regret throwing it away."

"You were following me?" Cornelius felt humiliated by the violation of his privacy.

"No. I mean, yes. But..."

"I'm going to have to report you."

"Please let me explain."

"Why? You were out of your territory by thousands of miles."

"Have it your way, but I invited you up here as a friendly gesture."

"Thanks, I guess," said Cornelius awkwardly. He was glad to have the tusk back, but suspicious. "Why were you in Bermuda anyway?"

"I was instructed to offer you assistance."

"Instructed?" Cornelius shook his head, agitated. "Who instructed you to...no, just forget it."

Kao pointed to the tusk. "May I ask what you were carving?"

"It's supposed to be a horse."

"Oh? Do you ride?"

"When I was alive everybody rode a horse."

Kao gestured to the skyline of Tokyo. "Do you want to fly around the city?"

"Maybe another day," said Cornelius. He politely explained that he had to return to the Dwelling, but he remained troubled, certain that Kao had an ulterior motive for returning the tusk.

14

Waiting atop Mount Fuji, boxed between the gray sky and the drab rain-pelted snow, preyed on Kao. It was an unpleasant reminder of standing outside the halls of the House of Representatives in Tokyo—for what seemed a lifetime—waiting for petitions to make it to the floor. Now, weeks of surveillance were ruined by the abrupt return of the carved tusk to Cornelius, and though unsure of the repercussions, it was no surprise when a khaki-colored mist appeared.

"Hello Kao," said Luboslaw, coalescing into form. "Pardon the intrusion. How was the rendezvous with Cornelius?"

"Disappointing," reported Kao. "He became suspicious when I returned the tusk."

Luboslaw scratched his prickly gray beard, grown long-ago when street-fighting against Nazis in Poland.

"What if he reports it to Ayodele?" Kao asked.

"The tusk is illegal—he will have no choice but to reconsider." Luboslaw turned to face the mountain. "You will try again?"

"Yes, sir."

Luboslaw reiterated how it was vital to have a number of options to stop Roger Mortimer, considered by the Provocateurs to be a radical Traditionalist, and that Cornelius Hoyt was such an option. Luboslaw pulled his cloak tight and stepped off the edge of the private Dwelling. "And Kao..."

"Yes?"

"You have served with honor." Luboslaw saluted.

Kao was deeply touched by the sign of respect.

"I...I want to..." Luboslaw waved away the words. "Please guard against betrayal."

"Yes, sir, I will."

15

As Cornelius approached the Dwelling two assignments emerged over the faux arteries and veins of his left forearm, and—fast becoming a habit—he tried to rub them away. He gobbled up a mouthful of snow and headed west, glancing down at the waves roiling the Atlantic Ocean.

The scroll on Seth Reitwiesner, thirty nine year-old man of Rhode Island, overwhelmed Cornelius. Seth had multiple health problems, including degenerative joint disease, intellectual developmental disorder, and a heart valve replacement. Cornelius figured a reaper with a history as a physician would be better suited to decode the medical jargon.

Cornelius arrived in Rhode Island and skulked about the ranch style house on 30 Cavalconte Road in Nooseneck. It had new kitchen appliances and a new leather loveseat and couch.

"Stop it!"

"Please stand up Seth. You can do it."

Cornelius followed the voices to an oversized bathroom. Seth sat in a wheelchair and two women were attempting to lift him onto the toilet. Cornelius watched Seth, thinking he was insane—he drooled, rocked back and forth and expressed no words, only noises.

"Damn it, get up!" yelled the younger woman.

Seth banged his forearm against his forehead, leaving an ugly bruise.

"Gisele, you can't talk like that," said the older woman firmly.

"But, Nancy, he's doing it on purpose."

"I know, trust me, I know," said Nancy. "Take a break, go have a cigarette." It thrilled Cornelius when Gisele picked up a towel, revealing ample cleavage.

"What about these laces Seth?" Nancy retied the sneakers. "You're big and strong, I know you can pivot to the toilet."

Seth moved to get up, but he fell, knocking Nancy to the floor and giving her a concussion. The situation deteriorated when Seth had a seizure and convulsed violently. It was perverse and disturbing to Cornelius. "What do I do?" he screeched—silent while invisible. He shut his eyes tight and lowered the scythe down on Seth.

A light snow falling over Maine seemed to alleviate the heavy stupor Cornelius felt after reaping the soul of Seth. He arrived in the town of Raymond and flew down the roads already covered with rock salt. On Mill Street, Frank Guerette walked down an aisle of the Rite-Aid Pharmacy wearing a black hooded sweatshirt. Cornelius settled on a windowsill cluttered with dusty sets of antique pestles and mortars. When the last customer exited the store Guerette ran up to the pharmacist, pointing a gun.

"Give me your oxycodone!"

"Okay, okay." Frightened, the pharmacist accidentally knocked over a display of lip balm. "Sorry, sorry."

"Hurry up!"

Cornelius shadowed Guerette as he ran out of the store with the drugs, jumped on a motorcycle and sped away. Cornelius pursued, impressed by the maneuverability of the vehicle. At a turn in the road Frank Guerette stopped and hid the motorcycle in a ditch and dashed into the woods, protected from the searchlights of a police helicopter by towering pine trees.

Before long, police and state troopers were following Guerette with trained dogs, while powerful flashlights caught glimpses of the young man running, weaving around the trees. At last, Guerette came to a stop, leaned against a tree and took an oxycodone.

Two minutes left, and Cornelius had a rush of ideas: a drug overdose, a self-inflicted gunshot, a long fall down a ravine. One minute. Guerette was trudging down a steep embankment toward a stream when he was tackled by a policeman. They tumbled down into the shallow river. Twelve seconds. The men were covered with mud as they wrestled, and a gun fell to the ground. A police dog tore at the suspect, and they separated for a moment. The policeman picked up the gun, but the men tangled again. Cornelius moved the gun so that it pointed at Guerette and pulled the trigger. The man collapsed, hemorrhaging from the abdomen.

Cornelius spirited to an isolated region and gulped cold water from a hole on a frozen pond; in the distance two ice fishermen cooked salmon on a small fire. He wanted to stay and roam the woods, but he needed to talk to Linnaeus.

Standing outside of Krubera Cave, Linnaeus ignored hail pounding the undulating terrain. Six people ran to a rusted van, seeking protection from the storm.

"Welcome my friend."

"What are you doing out here?"

"I'm keeping an eye on our mortal friends," said Linnaeus, pointing to the van.

The hail stopped. The explorers reemerge from the van. They regrouped and crawled down into the earth one by one, lowering ropes and backpacks. The dark cave immediately turned vertical, with no measured gradient. The explorers wore goggles and lighted helmets, and gradually rappelled downwards.

"I'm delighted you've come," said Linnaeus. "We have orders to move the RD."

"Move?" Cornelius imagined an exotic locale.

"We're currently 7,500 feet below the surface, and our explorer friends recently made it to 7,208 feet. I understand the Triumvirate is very upset mortals are invading every nook in the world. Anyway, I have to move the department to an area virtually blocked, located at a depth of 7,921 feet." He moved toward the entrance. "Do you have a few minutes to help?"

"Sure." The prospect of working again in the RD bothered Cornelius.

They went down the opening together, past the explorers, and after a brief pause to allow Linnaeus to examine an insect, they arrived at the office. The renovated RD was virtually bare. Linnaeus gathered up a few stray biographical scrolls. "If you would, please demolish the limestone workstations so they appear as natural piles of rock. It requires carving skills." He handed Cornelius a large rock with a sharpened edge to use as a tool.

"I'm just an amateur," Cornelius protested mildly.

"Nonsense, the dominoes you carved were exquisite," said Linnaeus. "It's an important precaution in case our speleologists get here before the limestone erodes."

"I'll give it a try." Cornelius pushed over one limestone drafting table, smashing it, and used the crude tool to chip away its straight edges. The work reminded him of constructing a wall at home to keep goats out of the vegetable garden. Almost imperceptibly, his left hand cramped. He was scared. What if the walrus tusk contained a residue of saltwater? The cramp eased, and he attributed the strange experience to dehydration. He put the tool down. "Linnaeus?"

"Yes?"

"I wanted to ask your opinion," said Cornelius, "about whether I should report something."

"You are unsure whether to follow the letter of the law or its spirit?"

"What do you mean?"

"I apologize for interrupting, please continue."

Cornelius fidgeted. "Okay, remember the tusk I told you about?"

"Yes, you were carving a horse."

"That's right. I threw it away."

"Were you unhappy with it?"

"Not exactly, I made a mistake on an assignment and Ayodele questioned my commitment."

"So you threw away it as a symbolic act."

"Yes, I guess, but..."

"And wish to have it back."

"Linnaeus, I have the tusk." Cornelius removed it from the secret pocket of the cloak and showed Linnaeus. "The problem is that another cadet saw me throw it away and retrieved it. He was spying on me!"

Linnaeus placed his hands together, as if to say a prayer. "Tell me, why would this cadet follow you, and why did he return the horse?"

"Why do you always ask me questions when I ask *you* a question?" Cornelius walked over to the vestibule. "I want advice!"

"You are right," said Linnaeus, softly. "My dear Sara often made the same observation." He sat down. "My advice is do not report the incident. Tell me, this cadet, can he be trusted?"

"He seemed harmless."

"Like he had good intentions?"

"Yes."

"Even down here at the RD, we understand that The Society of Death is at a crossroads." Linnaeus nodded. "You must be cautious. It's possible that this cadet may want to use you."

"Me?" Cornelius had steadfastly avoided the debate between the Provocateurs and Traditionalists, what Reverend Elliot would have mocked as "political intrigue."

"Beware, my friend," said Linnaeus, "lest you be deemed a pawn...and sacrificed."

16

A light drizzle fell over London. The new prime minster was handed a Harrods umbrella decorated with dogs to remind the electorate he owned a cocker spaniel, and to soften the fact he was a divorcee with no children. A make-up artist applied a hint of rouge to give a youthful quality to the sixty six year-old, and slightly mussed his coiffed hair to suggest a hardworking man. The PM waited for the cue to step out to a small 'x' marked on the street.

The chief of staff had leaked news of the safe release of the imprisoned Special Forces unit, and an adoring crowd waited outside 10 Downing Street. An officer with specialist protection indicated that the area was secure and the PM, code name Sage, was cleared to exit the residence.

"Thank you all for coming out today!" Mr. Lowe feigned spontaneity, but the words were rehearsed. He basked in the adulation.

"I want you to know…our soldiers are coming home!" Lowe paused to allow the applause to rise, and over the roar, yelled, "I want the world to know…I admire the courage and dignity of our armed forces!"

The crowd cheered wildly. Prime Minister Lowe turned deliberately to face a few soldiers present at the ceremony, and joined the applause. "It is altogether fitting that we salute our troops," he said, "for they represent the very best of Britain."

Lowe moved away from the group of reporters, using the umbrella as a walking stick, a gesture pundits suggested was calculated to reassure the markets he was no populist but a jaunty aristocrat who would protect the financial industry. He stepped up to the famous black door with the white number ten and its awkwardly aligned zero, and turned to face the people.

"I will take leave of you now…I will strive to serve the interests of Britain and its values and people. Let me say… it is a privilege to be your prime minister."

"Godspeed, sir!" hollered an elderly man from the assembled crowd.

"Thank you, Mr. Prime Minister!" squealed a toddler. The crowd waved small flags, distributed by an intern to the chief of staff.

As the lone surviving heir to one of the original partners of Jaguar, Harold Lowe inherited a fortune. He attended Eton and served in the army, receiving a wound in the Falls Curfew battle of 1971. As foreign secretary, he had aspired to the leadership position but committed a monumental breach of etiquette when he accidentally caused King William to trip as he toured a new hospital. The incident was replayed thousands and thousands of times. Although the young king handled it graciously—quipping to reporters that he had two royal left feet —the incident brought ridicule onto the royals and made Lowe a pariah.

The Royal Stumble—as it became known, ultimately caused Lowe to resign as foreign secretary. The scuttlebutt around London was that he would retire from politics, but Lowe stayed on as a Member of Parliament after the attack on the HMS *Albion* by Iran.

The crisis united Great Britain as Conservatives, and the majority of the Labour Party, demanded a military retaliation. Lowe was as outraged as the rest of the United Kingdom by the unprovoked attack on the British navy in the Persian Gulf, and hawkish by nature, it was out of character for him to publicly oppose—vehemently and without reservation—a military solution.

Lowe made a series of statements from the backbench that proved to be prophetic. He vociferously opposed retaliation, over jeers and taunting chants of "resign" and stubbornly insisted a true leader resisted the desire to exact revenge. He predicted a counterattack would be imprudent. Instead, he vaguely advocated, "a real solution."

The National Security Council implemented Operation Finest Hour, a limited military action designed to strike the Iranian Air Force base in Shiraz, the origin of the attack on the *Albion*. The operation was a catastrophe. It destroyed only one Iranian fighter jet, while two Royal Air Force Typhoons were shot down and the crew captured.

Lowe had articulated the risks of military intervention with clarity, and emerged from the crisis with a revived reputation.

An intangible Wall separated Grim Reapers from humanity, and protected the daily lives of mortals. Violation of the Wall was considered an incestuous mixing of the living and the dead, and the ultimate taboo. Nevertheless, when Mortimer saw an opportunity, he ignored the Wall and contacted Lowe.

It happened on the Serpentine Bridge in Hyde Park. Lowe, slightly drunk, had come to the park to avoid images of King William tripping—they seemed to be everywhere, at all times.

"Good evening," said Mortimer, pulling up his jacket collar to hide the ancient scars on his neck.

"Evening," said Lowe, curtly.

"The reflection of the moon off the lake is exquisite," observed Mortimer, "Do you suppose Queen Caroline enjoyed it?" he asked, aware the lake was constructed for the 18th century queen as part of a royal plan to improve Hyde Park.

"Yes, I should think so," said Lowe, glancing at the lake. "It is lovely."

Mortimer nurtured a conversation about the evolution of Hyde Park from a private hunting ground to the construction of The Grand Entrance. He wavered at breeching the Wall. There was no precedent for a conversation with a mortal about the existence of Grim Reapers, but with the help of dark energy, Mortimer succeeded.

"Sir, I understand you are an aficionado of Shakespeare," said Mortimer casually. It belied the conversation to come.

"Of course, I read the Bard to relax."

Mortimer knew he was lying, but ignored it. He halted and scanned the park. Raising an arm, he projected loudly to the stars, "The sense of death is most in apprehension..."

Lowe made a quizzical face. "Hamlet?"

"Measure for Measure," countered Mortimer, exhilarated at the prospect of breaking down the Wall. Having broached the subject of death, he saw no way to advance without first reassuring the mortal. "I will allow you to live."

"Excuse me?" Lowe hastily turned and headed toward a park exit.

Mortimer moved to block Lowe. "Please allow me to introduce myself. I am 3rd Baron Mortimer, 1st Earl of March. Grim Reaper 1st Tier."

Mortimer anticipated that the mortal would conclude he was insane, possibly violent, and attempt to flee. He prepared to provide incontrovertible proof that he was indeed a Grim Reaper, and pointed at a man walking along the path around the Serpentine. The man fell dead.

"Help!" screamed Lowe, running away.

Mortimer moved ahead toward a litter bin and kicked it over, knocking Lowe down.

"Calm yourself and listen," said Mortimer. "You learned reapers were a myth, but myths have origins in truth."

Lowe squeezed his eyes shut. "I mixed alcohol and medication. It's a hallucination."

"Sir, I *am* real." Mortimer attempted to be reassuring.

Lowe quivered but recovered sufficiently to sit, leaning against the litter receptacle. He wiped away mucous with a handkerchief embossed HL. "I beg your pardon," he said, panting. "No offense, but I find it hard to accept you are who you claim to be."

"Fair enough, Mr. Lowe." Mortimer contemplated a way to authenticate, beyond spiriting and reaping, but dismissed the notion of telling Lowe that it was *he* who caused the king to trip on the hospital tour. "I seem to recall when you were sixteen and driving around the back roads of Warwickshire in a 1968 Jaguar XKE Coupe—beautiful machine, ah, what was I saying oh, yes…you killed a man."

Already soiled, Lowe vomited. He had told no one about the accident. No parent, mate, or reverend. The local newspaper had reported it as a hit-and-run, and that the victim was a young Jamaican émigré with no family. The police had conducted an inquiry, but there were no witnesses and no leads. "How do you know about that?" Lowe wept uncontrollably.

"I was watching you."

Mortimer observed Lowe over many years, as he had several mortals with the potential to achieve leadership positions, and noted several indicators of depravity, including the relative ease with which he shed guilt over committing vehicular manslaughter, and how well he managed alcoholism, extramarital affairs, and devious financial arrangements.

"Don't kill me!" beseeched Lowe.

Mortimer was disappointed when Lowe collapsed unconscious that evening on the Serpentine Bridge, but he was sufficiently encouraged to dial 999 on the mobile for medical assistance.

Mortimer observed Lowe over the next several days, appalled to find that he frequently became inebriated and regressed to incredulity and terror, or bounced erratically between megalomania and depression. It demanded patience, but Mortimer slowly convinced Lowe that if he cooperated, he would become prime minster of Great Britain.

In addition to Lowe, Mortimer monitored Hugo Cardiff. Another mortal with the prerequisites to ascend to a leadership position, born of a wealthy family, he excelled at school and was a popular politician. Unfortunately, Cardiff lacked ambition, and accepted an appointment to the House of Lords. Another man, a young mortal, Aaron Thatcher, grand-nephew of Margaret Thatcher, held potential, but he was underage.

Mortimer fantasized about controlling a U.S. President, but he had limited options in the Unites States. A Representative from Virginia, a gifted orator and handsome enough to have once modeled, lost viability when he was caught with a male prostitute. Another man, a retired admiral and hero of the U.S. victory over China in the skirmish over Taiwan, vacillated over pursuing a political career.

Fortunately, Harold Lowe survived the meeting on the Serpentine Bridge. He proved resilient, staying on as a member of parliament. When informed by Mortimer that Finest Hour would fail, Lowe confidently opposed the mission, guaranteed that he would be vindicated.

The failure of the mission wounded the economy of Great Britain, as oil prices skyrocketed and caused a severe recession. It led to violent protests throughout the United Kingdom. Crowds marched on 10 Downing Street and Buckingham Palace, threatening the foundation of the government, and though troops were deployed, many were sympathetic to the protesters. It terrified the establishment, and tempted Mortimer. It would have been easy, probably a mere random shot by a guard, to push the crowd to attack the palace, but he understood that sometimes restraint led to prodigious reapings. It was hard for Mortimer, but he had allowed the protests to subside and felt vindicated when Lowe secured the position of prime minister.

Inside 10 Downing Street, Prime Minster Lowe politely requested privacy to draft a speech on reducing corporate taxes. He sauntered across the black and white checkered marble floor and walked up the main staircase to a soundproof private office, leaving the door ajar. He sat on a reupholstered leather chair, an antique from the days of William Pitt, lit a cigar and poured a brandy. Through the bullet-proof window he noticed birds flying in and out of a birdhouse precariously attached to a branch of an oak tree. The door to the private office shut hard.

Mortimer materialized on the window sill. "Evening, Mr. Prime Minister."

"Evening, 1st Earl."

Mortimer pulled down the window shade. "Are you ready to proceed?"

"I believe I am," said Lowe. "Our meetings have developed a reassuring routine."

"Excellent."

The PM shifted in the deep leather chair and shivered from the sudden drop in temperature of the room. Mortimer requested that he put out the cigar, but he allowed Lowe to keep the brandy and enjoyed it vicariously.

"I am here to discuss with you the next stage of our partnership." Mortimer used the word "partnership" to soothe the ego of the PM.

"The next stage? But, I am already prime minister."

"You test my patience, Mr. Lowe," snarled Mortimer, riled by the vanity of the mortal. "It may surprise you to learn, but you are merely part of a greater objective."

Mortimer came to Downing Street to update the PM that moments ago he had reaped the British ambassador in Tehran under suspect circumstances. The intent was to give Lowe an excuse to order the launch of a precision-guided bomb at Tehran "to restore British honor" and set the stage for a regional conflict. Nonetheless, Mortimer concluded it would be best if Lowe learned of the news from the embassy and reacted spontaneously.

"Right," said Lowe, sipping the brandy. "I have a few suggestions to tighten my grip on power."

Mortimer listened with barely masked impatience as the prime minister listed a set of ordinary issues, but interrupted when Lowe specifically requested the "elimi-nation" of the leader of a coal strike. "Mr. Prime Minister, these are trivial matters, soon you will have great powers. I must go now, carry on."

It pained Mortimer, but he grudgingly accepted that the arc of the universe bent toward justice, an observation credited to a mortal, Dr. Martin Luther King, Jr. It would require an extraordinary power to invert the arc, and Mortimer had faith that the only available means was an alliance with dark energy. He understood that he would have to play a subservient role. It was a steep price to pay, but he paid it in order to rule The Society of Death. He had expected to work with a tangible expression of dark energy, but it was remote, beyond the bitter cold of a cell in the Tower of London, beyond the icy touch of a Grim Reaper. It possessed an underlying coercion.

He would halfheartedly kneel in an undiscovered cave under Nottingham Castle and silently make "requests" of dark energy, disturbed by its demand to genuflect. The master plan, the grand scheme, came together while he was dormant. It was simple and unique, the traditional markers of success, but on a fantastic scale, designed to trump the greatest accomplishments of Ayodele. He dubbed it Operation Balghstaf—a word that harkened back to Middle English and captured the essence of the mission. Mortimer swore to *bludgeon* the mortal race. He wanted to achieve the greatest Event ever and reap a robust 13% of the world population, or approximately 975,000,000 mortal souls. He even dared to hope Balghstaf would achieve one billion deaths.

The news of the sudden death of Ambassador Geoffrey Lockhart in Tehran reverberated inside 10 Downing Street. Lowe prepared a statement, careful to include condolences to Mrs. Lockhart and the gratitude of the nation for decades of public service, and demands for an exhaustive investigation. He would conclude with a dramatic "promise" to restore British prestige. The conjecture that the ambassador was poisoned intensified when the Iranians delayed an autopsy by a British medical examiner.

Mortimer had used an especially lethal version of polonium-210, a toxin Iran was capable of acquiring from Russia. He watched the prime minister deliver the statement, and satisfied by the speech, decided to visit Buckingham Palace; amused by the fact he was a distant relative of the royal family.

Standing on the famous balcony of the palace, Mortimer imagined wearing a crimson cloak during a coronation attended by the outstanding Grim Reapers of the day, it would be a glorious celebration, and include a banquet and ritualistic reapings of select mortals.

King Mortimer, intoned dark energy, *King Mortimer.*

17

A herd of African forest elephants dug into the ground to get minerals, one dove underwater to get at the rich soil of a riverbed.

Sebastian checked the time on his railroad pocket watch. He constructed it over decades of tinkering with spare parts and observing watch makers. "Great Spirit of the Forest Elephant!" he beckoned, impatient with the tardy spirit.

The vaporous Great Spirit of the Forest Elephant coalesced as gentle as dew, and stood on the opposite bank of the river waving its tail. "Greetings."

"Thank you." Sebastian bowed. "I am honored to stand among such a magnificent herd." He was genuinely awed by the creatures, but transitioned to negotiations. "The soul I have today lived as an altruistic mortal devoted to the welfare of animals."

"Indeed."

"The soul operated an animal rescue shelter and lived a vegan lifestyle. We believe he merits a life among your majestic kind."

"I agree the mortal lived a very commendable life. I have no doubt that most species would accept such a soul." The Great Spirit charged across the river to Sebastian. "But, I reject it!"

"Respectfully, Great Spirit...why?" Refusals rarely happened, and Sebastian would have to explain it to Linnaeus.

"Because," explained the Great Spirit, "I remember an incident involving the grandfather of the mortal."

"Are you holding the sins of the grandfather against the grandson?"

"Yes!" trumpeted the Great Spirit of the Forest Elephant. "The grandfather came to my homeland and shot eleven illustrious elephants with a double-barreled rifle. The mortal came upon two families, and without reason, shot them to death. The fool posed for a photograph leaning against one carcass as cavalierly as if he were leaning against a rock. I then followed the caravan of mortals to a ship and observed as they used a crane to load the carcasses!"

"I respect your decision Great Spirit." Sebastian accepted the memory of the Great Spirit of the Forest Elephant as gospel, and with no way to negotiate out of the impasse, bid farewell. "I am honored to have experienced your presence," he said shamefaced, for as a mortal he had cleaned dead animals off the cowcatcher of trains.

"Thank you," said the Great Spirit. "You are welcomed to return in the future."

Sebastian walked invisible among the herd, admiring the great beasts before embarking on the trip back to the Replanting Department. The elephants flapped their ears at the buzz of a materializing 1st Tier. The highly irregular visit concerned Sebastian, and he wondered if the failed negotiation was a serious problem instead of a temporary inconvenience. "To what do I owe the honor?" he asked.

The 1st Tier squirted a stream of saltwater at Sebastian, who fell to the ground agonizing. "Interesting how your face now resembles your damaskeened pocket watch," said the perpetrator, before dousing Sebastian and dissolving what remained of him to a pile of iron filings.

18

Reapers of the Queuing Station had limited spiriting privileges, but Houdon risked a trip to the Dwelling. He landed on the skerry, appalled by its sterility. While the Queuing Station was no field of lavender, it had ambiance, a kind of brute architecture. Centuries earlier, souls waited outdoors to be replanted, but population growth and ever-increasing urbanization squeezed out available areas, necessitating that the Queuing Station be relocated. The abandoned quarries under Paris once supplied the raw material to construct many buildings, including the Cathedral of Notre Dame, and many of the old caves were long forgotten. The Queuing Station positioned its headquarters in a catacomb filled with bones Parisians haphazardly piled up over the centuries. They used an immense limestone pillar as a hub, and tunnels radiated outward to form orderly queues.

Houdon ignored the unpleasant terrain. He was determined to warn Cornelius, while simultaneously protecting the plot he helped Luboslaw design to thwart Roger Mortimer.

Houdon was an original Provocateur, present at the formation of the group during the Time Protocol in the shadows of the Cliffs of Pico Bolivar. He witnessed how the host, 2nd Tier Charles Baudelaire, circled the cliffs and acknowledged the dignitaries from around the world. "Let us rejoice in the ardor of our work. We have come together to the detriment of the mortal race and will leave here with the *time* to do our work." Baudelaire memorably kicked over a cairn, and shouted, "The devil holds the strings!"

1st Tier Pedro Alvarez, veteran of the Spanish Inquisition, argued with a sing-song voice for the traditional method of organizing time. "Brothers, our beloved Medhat has served us faithfully for centuries." The words echoed among the cliffs. "Named to honor our venerable Grim Reaper of ancient Egypt...We must revere tradition!" When the friar shut the over-sized Grim Reaper Canon, a yellow-brown dust arose, residue of mustard gas from World War I. Houdon recalled how the assembly of reapers—anonymity protected by drawn hoods—stood when Alvarez raised both hands and implored: "Long live the Medhat!"

The Medhat was the basic unit of time (equal to 9.09 minutes) and based on the period required for the mythological Grim Reaper to spirit around the Earth. However, growing demands on The Society of Death strained its effectiveness, and many felt a new standard of time was needed, one immediately familiar to younger reapers.

Houdon witnessed Charles Tallow counter the arguments of Alvarez.

"As a mortal of recent times, I tell you quite unequivocally that superstitions are receding and knowledge and skepticism are valued. It is incumbent upon us to use a system suitable to the age we reap. The increasing mortal population demands we use a standardized structure of time to manage our affairs." Tallow crisscrossed the cliffs slowly as if pacing in a courtroom, and reached up to adjust a tie he no longer wore, an old habit. "I want to say… Saint Alvarez, I respect you."

"Gracias, brother reaper."

"All the same," drawled Tallow, "I have a question."

"Sí?"

"Saint Alvarez, I beg your patience...I believe you have made the case to adopt the mortal time system."

"Señor, you will not persuade the esteemed reapers among us with a fabrication."

"*Saint* Alvarez," said Tallow with studied emphasis, "why do you accept the honorarium of saint...no doubt, deserved...when it was bestowed by mortals?"

"I...I..."

Tallow suggested if an honorarium of mortalkind was valued by a 1st Tier, it seemed reasonable to use a "system" invented by mortals. He explained in an Ohioan accent how reapers use English as the official language just as mortals do when conducting international business. He pointed out examples of the excellent tools invented by mortals to organize time—advanced atomic clocks and Coordinated Universal Time—and alluded to the irony of using a technique designed by mortals to improve the work of Grim Reapers. He concluded by referring to the logistical problems faced by reapers in a world of 7,500,000,000 souls, thereby making the need for a standardized measurement of time seem self-evident.

Alvarez pointed at Tallow, "Woe unto ye, lawyer..."

A rumbling of 'yeas' from the dark choir of reapers drowned out Alvarez. The motion to officially replace the Medhat with Coordinated Universal Time passed (reapers were permitted to use local time zones).

The adoption of the mortal time system inspired an informal group of reapers to organize as the Provocateurs, unified by the shared belief that Grim Reapers had to adapt to the modern world. The existence of the Provocateurs led to the formation of the Traditionalists. They believed that only by strengthening the old ways would The Society of Death be restored to the glorious days of the Dark Ages, when reapers accounted for 77.6% of deaths; it now stood at a historical low of 23.1%.

Houdon found the young cadet skimming stones across the calm ocean. "Bonjour, Corn."

"Hi," said Cornelius. He ingested a handful of snow, the various states of water were a pleasure to reapers;

liquid rated most popular, snow second, steam a distant third.

Houdon dug at the ground with his heel. "Tough place to farm, eh?"

"Barely a pail of soil."

"My friend, I have only a few moments," said Houdon, eager to get back to the Queuing Station. "I have come to warn you about Roger Mortimer."

"What have I got to do with Mortimer?"

"I will explain. He and I were...how you say... contemporains."

"You were contemporaries?"

"Yes," said Houdon. "You have to understand our adversary."

"*Our* adversary?"

"I align with the Provocateurs." Houdon had grown impatient with unaligned reapers. "Don't you?"

"I'm just a cadet." Cornelius picked up his scythe. "I only want..."

"Listen to what I have to tell you."

Houdon told Cornelius how, as a mortal, the duly imprisoned Mortimer escaped from the Tower of London, fled to France and raised an army. It grieved Houdon to talk about how bloodthirsty troops led by Mortimer pillaged estates throughout France, including the one he worked. He explained how Mortimer invaded England and deposed King Edward II. The king was executed, and

Mortimer ruled with a vengeance, illegally appropriating estates throughout Britain and Ireland.

"Why do I have to learn about Mortimer?" Cornelius wiped the blade of his scythe clean.

"We have reason to believe he will attempt a catastrophic worldwide Event."

"But the actions of a 1st Tier..."

"Oh, mon dieu!" Houdon stomped down on the ground and charged towards Cornelius. "He set the Great Fire of London in 1666!" Houdon regretted telling the young reaper. He saw the rage in Cornelius and sympathized— after all, he still wanted to hurt Mortimer for ransacking the old estate and murdering his friends, but he had tempered his anger over the centuries.

Enraged, Cornelius heaved his scythe as if were a javelin. It landed on a patch of ice and slid toward the edge of the skerry. Houdon raced towards the scythe, but it hit the water. There was scarcely a splash, only a plume of smoke and a stench of rotting flesh.

"My scythe!" screamed Cornelius. "What have I done?"

Houdon guided Cornelius away from the edge, toward the chambers.

"What about my scythe?"

"I will get you another one," said Houdon, filled with self-loathing.

"Blades are synchronized to individual cadets," whispered Cornelius, almost incoherent as he walked unsteadily.

"I'm sorry," said Houdon. "I only meant to warn you about Mortimer."

"You'd better get back to the Queuing Station."

"What will you do?"

"I don't know," said Cornelius checking both forearms. He feared a sudden visit from Ayodele or Páll, knowing he had no way to complete an assignment.

"I have a suggestion," said Houdon. It was fraught with risk, but he felt he owed it to Cornelius. "Go visit Kao."

"Kao?"

"He might know someone who can help you." Houdon realized the longer he stayed, the greater the danger. He had already done enough damage. "Au revoir, mon ami."

19

Cornelius fumed. Rage and resentment had replaced unremitting guilt about the Great Fire of London. He spent over three hundred fifty years exiled at the RD for a crime he did not commit, working in the confines of the Krubera Cave as a bureaucrat, completing replantings while the world became an exhilarating place of change.

Five mortals approached the skerry on an inflatable raft and came ashore. Cornelius slumped down to the ground and watched the group unpack a small propane stove. He had no desire to be brutally expelled, and considered telling Ayodele the truth, but that would implicate Houdon. There were no real options, but to go to Mount Fuji. If Kao were a Provocateur, he might have links to a Grim Reaper capable of replacing a lost scythe.

He spirited over Eastern Europe, tracing the Pechora River south towards the Ural Mountains. He landed and drank from the Chusovaya River; a rock face of a cliff over the river bore a disturbing resemblance to Roger Mortimer.

Cornelius followed the tracks of the Trans-Siberian Railroad. It was a lonely trip, but skies brightened over

Siberia and he accelerated with a warm southwesterly airstream. He was miserable, replaying the death of Dr. ZZ and the Expulsion of Skowron, and weakened by the hours and hours of travel without the rejuvenating power of a dormant state. He flew over the Great Wall of China, traced its route to a remote mountainous region, and rested in a woodland area.

A glorious Japanese sunrise welcomed Cornelius to Mount Fuji. He searched the snow covered mountainside, and found the path leading to the hollow and the private Dwelling. He anxiously searched the crag for Kao, known to carry a heavy workload. Cornelius moved down a short narrow passage leading to an artificial perpendicular tunnel, the wind blew a range of low notes through the slight aperture. He spirited up to the chamber, and wiped away the dew on the exterior shell. He fell backward—Kao was a woman!

Shocked, he stared at Kao—naked with curving hips and tiny breasts—captivated by the sight. As the chamber slowly opened, Cornelius turned and faced a wall.

"Cornelius, please let me explain." Kao covered up with a cloak. "I am a woman…I mean, obviously, but what you have to understand…I mean, you probably do, as a woman I represent a profound challenge to The Society of Death, but…"

He barely heard the words, overwhelmed by the upheaval of last twelve hours—the visit by Houdon with the news about Mortimer and the Great Fire, dire warnings about a worldwide plot, losing the scythe, and now the revelation about Kao. Most disturbing were the physical changes, the hand cramp at Krubera, the growing desire he felt to be among people and the strange stirrings when he saw Kao naked. Exhausted, he collapsed and fell down the vertical tunnel, hit the ground and rolled onto the crag at the edge of the hollow, and staggered down the path on the side of the mountain.

Kao swiftly approached. "Are you all right?"

A light snow began to fall. Cornelius sat on rock.

"I will get you a cup of Universal Elixir."

"Okay."

Kao abruptly dropped to the ground and gestured to Cornelius to get down. Two mortals had reached the Dwelling, one had a camera.

"What do we do?"

"We have to get out of here," said Kao. "I have a safe house."

As the voices of the mortals grew louder, they spirited away.

20

When Luboslaw recruited Kao, he immediately established a secret hideaway. He anticipated that Kao would be revealed to be a woman and summarily executed to deter any further attempts to fundamentally alter death. He had witnessed covert plans unravel hundreds of times, and he cared about the welfare of Kao as he would a daughter.

He established the original hideaway on the tallest of the rock formations known as Three Brothers in Avacha Bay of the Kamchatka Peninsula. Luboslaw selected the site to honor two younger brothers, decorated pilots of the Polish Air Force, killed in the Battle of Britain. Yet, as much as he valued the symbolism, Luboslaw decided to change the contingency plan. The rock formations were remote, but typical of a GR locale—a distinctive natural formation virtually inaccessible by mortals—and therefore predictable.

In 1939, Luboslaw was a thirty four year-old bachelor, a mechanic—expert under the hood of any car or truck, and a dedicated lifeguard at a swim camp. Everything changed when the Nazis invaded Poland.

He learned guerilla warfare tactics as a soldier in the Polish Underground and excelled as a saboteur, a specialist at derailing trains and breaking supply lines. Following a raid to get medical supplies, Luboslaw promised a dying friend that he would protect a local orphanage for girls. When the orphanage was hit during a German aerial bombardment on Polish supply lines, Luboslaw was suicidal with guilt. As a reaper, he vowed to honor the girls by reducing the number of Excruciating Deaths suffered by women.

Luboslaw determined Kamchatka was acceptable geographically, but instead of the unique formation of Three Brothers, he situated the safe house among mortals in the village of Klyuchi. He assembled a prefabricated steel home one mile beyond the town, and stocked it with basic tools and simple furniture. Next, he turned to the problem of Tracking. An innovation designed to protect the integrity of death from inexperienced or incompetent reapers, Tracking made hiding impossible. Or so it seemed. Luboslaw challenged three trusted 3rd Tiers to beat the system.

Myles, sixteen when he died in a skateboarding accident, temporarily avoided Tracking by hiding in a nuclear submarine. He remained undetectable while the submarine was submerged under saltwater, but he was revealed when the sub returned to port and opened its hatch.

Eddie, a former actor recruited when the flying apparatus of a theater malfunctioned, managed to delay detection. He temporarily confounded the exulted olfactory and auditory abilities possessed by GRs by hiding under the platform of the Canal Street subway station in Manhattan with its clamor of trains and sickening odors.

Miloš, diagnosed as a schizophrenic when mortal and alleviated of the ailment as a reaper, hit upon the ideal solution. Aware of the reapers inability to change the natural world, Miloš covered up from head to toe with a natural extract: argan oil. He went undetected standing on the Eiffel Tower practically in reach of reapers hard at work at the Queuing Station. The successful evasion of Tracking provided Luboslaw with vital intelligence, and he rewarded Miloš with a sentimental artifact, a fuel hose from a flamethrower he used during World War II.

Fortunately, the improved safe house on Kamchatka was operational when Luboslaw heard about the disappearance of Kao and Cornelius. Luboslaw volunteered to lead the search for the "criminals", confident he would be able to impede the hunt long enough to help Kao.

21

Cornelius glanced up at the rafters of the cabin. The contraption resembled a giant steel jaw-trap. Aside from the table and two chairs, the cabin contained all the basics: a sink, wood-burning stove, refrigerator and a rusted generator. "What about a supply of Universal Elixir?" he asked.

Kao pointed out the window at a round tank that collected rainwater, beyond the tank the forests of Kamchatka seemed to go on forever.

"Hurry," said Kao, opening a tall cabinet filled with bottles of argan oil. "We have to apply argan oil over our bodies, and put on clothes made of hemp, soy, and bamboo."

"Wait...what?" He turned as Kao removed her cloak.

"The natural oils and materials will shield us."

"I don't understand?"

"I was told by a reliable source we may be able to block Tracking with these oils and clothes."

Cornelius searched the cabin, hoping to find another method to avoid detection, mortified to undress with a woman in the room. He hastily removed the cloak and poured globs of oil over each shoulder and spread it rapidly. He picked up the clothes piled on a chair, and with difficulty put on the unfamiliar undergarments, tripping as he pulled up the pants.

"What do we do if those mountain climbers explore the Dwelling and find your scythe?"

"Both are unnatural, and will quickly fade away without a trace."

"What about the photographs?"

"We are only visible at the precise moment of a reaping a soul, therefore they will appear blank." Kao adjusted her blouse, and buttoned it up to the neck. "The real problem is the direct Sighting by the climbers."

"They'll think you were a hiker."

"You know as well I do, it will result in my Expulsion."

"I'm sorry," said Cornelius. "It's my fault."

"I accept responsibility. It was my chamber." Kao counted the bottles of argan oil. "I calculate we have enough oil to last six months."

"Six months!"

"We have each lost our scythe, and..."

"And you're a woman." Cornelius immediately regretted how indignant he sounded. "Um, how do you know about this grease?"

"Argan oil," clarified Kao. "I was prepared to escape by a Provocateur."

Cornelius was curious about the identity of the Provocateur, but was afraid to ask.

"We have to come up with a believable story," said Kao. "I suggest we pose as a couple. We have to gather food and pretend to use the outhouse."

"Sure, okay." Cornelius tied the laces on a pair of boots, impressed by the workmanship. He picked up the cloaks and lit a match.

Kao insisted Cornelius stop and blew out the match; he had forgotten the combustibility of the cloaks. Instead, he saturated them with argan oil and stuffed them into a hemp satchel.

"Typical," she said, shaking her head.

"What?"

"You could have *folded* the cloaks."

"Are you serious?"

Kao smiled.

The absolute darkness of night in Kamchatka reminded Cornelius of colonial times. The one lantern in the cabin emitted a pale light; it seemed to heighten the sense of danger.

Cornelius was tempted to sleep outdoors but Kao insisted that posing as a couple included sleeping together. It was a strange turn to be invited to bed by a woman. At seventeen, he ached to lay with buxom Susannah Parsons. Now he was guilt-ridden by the desire he had to be with Kao. Somehow though, a puritan ethic was irrelevant when you were dead. He got under the covers.

They kept on their hemp pants and shirts, ignoring the heavy cotton pajamas in the trunk that would require changing again. Cornelius lay perfectly still, afraid to accidentally touch Kao. It felt strange to rest lying down wearing clothes; he had grown accustomed standing up naked. He pulled up the wool blanket, last time he used one it smelled of coffee and pine—the scents of home.

For a moment, Cornelius was in the Dwelling, naked within a chamber. Realization came in a flash. He was in a cheap, metal shed hiding out with limited chances of survival, and lying next to a woman. As he got up, noise from the rickety bed awakened Kao.

"Sorry," he said.

"Ohayo."

"Ohio?"

"Ohayo," repeated Kao, getting up and moving to the tall cabinet. "It is a traditional Japanese greeting."

Cornelius made the bed, a chore he had as a boy. It was reassuring.

"We have to cover up." Kao retrieved two bottles of argan oil and handed one to Cornelius.

"Do we have to?"

"Yes. We have to be protected at all times."

"All over?"

"Yes...everywhere," she said shyly.

They turned around and slathered on the argan oil. Its mild nut scent smelled like autumn. When Cornelius finished and re-dressed, he inspected a shelf of tools— satisfied to find a hammer, a box of nails, screwdrivers, a saw, and a Swiss Army knife. He went outside and started to gather kindling.

Kao came out of the cabin. "What are you doing?"

"Getting kindling," said Cornelius, holding up a few sticks.

"For what purpose?"

"Kindling builds a fire."

"Oh, I understand," she said. "Mortals would have a fire burning and smoke coming out of the stovepipe." Cornelius noticed how the sunshine on her face high- lighted tiny freckles across her cheeks and the subtle curve of her eyelashes. It was hard to imagine in retrospect that he never suspected Kao was a woman.

Back to the cabin, Cornelius filled the wood stove with the kindling and built a fire, a puff of smoke streamed out of the chimney. "Okay, what do we do next?" he asked, sit- ting down. "Make an imaginary breakfast?"

"I have no idea," said Kao. "We have nothing to do. No books to read and we dare not spirit over the peninsula."

"How about we hike?" Cornelius got up and searched the cabin.

"You mean, survey the region?"

"Yes, exactly." Cornelius grabbed the Swiss Army knife and a brush hook hanging on a wall, excited at the prospect of forging a trail. Kao stood back from the sharp tool. "It'll cut a path," he explained, appraising the blade.

Although unaffected by the cold, they put on winter coats to keep up appearances. Cornelius enjoyed hacking out a trail from the thick underbrush, a crumpled flyer describing a lost German shepherd named Orochi was the only evidence of civilization in the virtually untouched forest.

Kao examined a pine cone. "I wish I had some paper to document my observations."

"I saw a notepad and a pencil on a shelf in the kitchen."

"Oh good, thank you."

Amid trees and lakes and outcroppings of rocks, they came upon the small village of Klyuchi. It had no town hall, fire department, or library, just houses scattered haphazardly and a nearby Russian military base. Men worked on cars, some unloaded lumber from trucks, and a group of women minded children playing on swing-sets made of wood. A Russian army helicopter flew overhead, reminding Cornelius of the risks of failing to behave as mortals. They decide to return to the security of the cabin.

Kao swept away the gathered dust and dirt, and then sat to make a detailed sketch of the pine cone. Cornelius found a hatchet and removed the branches of an overgrown willow that blocked the window. Next, he climbed up a tree and moved onto the roof of the cabin to chop away branches hanging over the chimney pipe. He tossed the branches down to the ground and sat on the roof, plagued by the memory of an assignment in Virginia.

At the Albemarle District Court in Charlottesville, Cornelius watched a district attorney prosecute Will Reilly, successful landscape architect and owner of VirginLand of Charlottesville. William Joseph Reilly—the prosecutor always referred to the man by his full name—was accused of conspiring to kill the husband of Veronica Thibodaux, the woman with whom he was having an affair. The case against the Reilly was strong until Cornelius took the soul of the district attorney. The case subsequently fell apart and Reilly was acquitted. Later, Reilly murdered Veronica Thibodaux. Cornelius regretted reaping the district attorney, sure that he would have successfully prosecuted Reilly and prevented the subsequent murder.

Cornelius wondered how many other reapings were similarly "contagious."

They hiked daily. Cornelius marked trees to avoid duplicate treks and to stay oriented without spiriting. He stopped complaining about the cabin or wondering how long they would have to wait to be rescued. Kao passed the days making detailed sketches of eagles, otters, foxes, and of the mountains and hot springs. Cornelius only wished they were able to enjoy it without the constant fear of Expulsion.

After weeks of cautious hikes, they decided to venture several miles beyond the cabin. The rivers were thawing and the abundance of fish amazed Cornelius. They crossed one with a strong current, and Kao held her notepad high to keep it dry and moved to the riverbank to sit.

"I imagine Carl Linnaeus would appreciate the flora and fauna of Kamchatka," she said.

"You're right." Cornelius picked up a bone at the edge of the river, wondering if it would be solid enough to carve. He peeked over Kao's shoulder at her drawing of a bear. "Linnaeus would certainly appreciate your ability to draw."

"I have a model," she said, pointing downriver with the pencil.

Cornelius instinctively leaned back when he saw an enormous brown bear feasting on a salmon.

Kao pulled out a small, stringy root from the ground and made a bracelet. "I have to tell you something."

"Okay."

"It may upset you," she said, slipping the bracelet onto his wrist.

"What is it?"

"I followed you twice."

"Twice?"

"The second occurrence was at the airport in Delaware."

"When I reaped the soul of Dr. ZZ?"

"Yes, I delayed the ambulance by causing it to swerve."

"Why? I had the Event under control. I made him suffer an Excruciating Death!"

Kao stood and put away the notepad and pencil. "Please, try to understand," she said softly. "Those few minutes were crucial. If the EMTs had arrived any sooner they might have saved Dr. ZZ."

Cornelius bristled. "Why was it important to you?"

"As part of an overall strategy to involve you with the Provocateurs, you had to succeed as cadet."

"Is that why you invited me to Mount Fuji after the workshop?"

"Yes, but..."

It hurt to learn that Kao had contacted him as part of a plan. He dropped the bone into river, the tiny boat floated away.

"My contact will come and rescue us soon." Kao stood and placed her hands on his shoulders. "We have to survive. We have important roles to play."

"What roles?" he asked, calmed to the core by her touch.

"I have no details."

"And you're willing to risk your existence?"

"Of course," said Kao, "to protect the mission."

"It's hard to imagine I have a role."

"It is because of your relationship to Roger Mortimer."

"Damn it, him again," said Cornelius. "Listen, I know he caused the Great Fire, I don't care anymore."

"May I ask you a question?"

"Sure," he said, reluctantly.

"Do you know how you were recruited?"

"I died of smoke inhalation." Cornelius vaguely recalled that it happened in a barn.

"May I tell you more?"

He guzzled water from a canteen. "Okay."

Kao spoke softly of the Event that lead to his death, about how a fire raced down a row of houses to the stables in the corner of the village.

"Now I remember," he said. "I went to rescue Arabella and saw a man standing in the hayloft."

"Who was the man?"

"I don't know, probably a neighbor. I went to help, but when I got to the ladder he was gone. I tried to get Arabella out, but the loft collapsed and killed her." Cornelius jumped up. "It was Mortimer!"

22

Linnaeus worked hard to recreate the Taxonomy of Souls on a wall in the new RD office. It was impossible to get any sort of paint down the tiny crevices leading in and out of the cave, but he had invented a unique paste that adhered to the damp limestone wall.

As he had in the 18th century when he established a classification system for animals, plants and minerals, Linnaeus produced a classification system for souls—he called it the *Systema Själ*. The purpose was to apply scientific rigor to replantings. However, organizing the taxonomy proved to be a daunting task, with perpetual revisions and a frustrating degree of subjectivity. Ultimately, Linnaeus decided on six classes of souls:

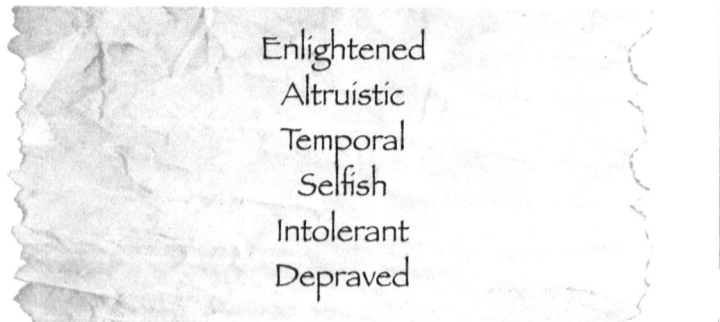

Enlightened
Altruistic
Temporal
Selfish
Intolerant
Depraved

Rewriting the details of the Taxonomy of Souls was a challenge. Each class of souls contained several orders based on specific traits, but the work helped Linnaeus deal with the losses of Kalidasa and Hale.

Kalidasa, GR-RD/1, an Indian writer from the 5th century, existed for a long, healthy deathspan of 1,607 years. Linnaeus had always depended on Kalidasa to keep replantings on schedule and for good conversation. He missed him terribly.

GR-RD/2 Hale was destroyed during an Allowance to Act Mortal. Hale had always loved aquariums and traveled across the world to tour the San Francisco Bay Aquarium. While the aquarium was closed, Hale, apparently unable to wait any longer, spirited past locked doors by way of the pipes straight into a tank of saltwater.

The RD was dangerously understaffed, and now GR-RD/4 Sebastian was late returning from negotiations with the Great Spirit of the Forest Elephant. Linnaeus worried about the normally punctual Sebastian, formerly a 19th century railroad conductor at the Belt Railroad of Chicago.

The Replanting Department typically required thirty years to replant a soul. Linnaeus wondered whether it were possible to maintain the quality of placements *and* stay on schedule. The list included:

419	earthquake victims from an Armenian village
1,089	causalities from a terrorist attack in Dubai
27	infant fatalities in Russia from contaminated milk powder
8,132	victims of a drought in Africa
2	murdered Tibetan Monks
1	drug overdose of an American singer

It was a tremendous amount of work, and Linnaeus anticipated protracted negotiations with the various Great Spirits as an increasing number of species refused to accept the obstreperous souls of Homo sapiens. He contemplated reclassifying the human race as *Homo fatuus*— foolish man.

"What am I to do with so many souls?" Linnaeus asked rhetorically.

"How about we replant them as krill," suggested Russell, appearing from around a corner.

"I am unwilling to be expedient with souls!"

"But, we're overworked," countered Russell. "In the past, many were bundled."

"By 'in the past' do you mean to say, 'traditionally'?" asked Linnaeus pointedly, sniffing a political bias. He insisted RD Team Members be categorically apolitical.

"No, sir."

"Excellent," said Linnaeus, unconvinced; Russell was a conniver. "Now, I need pradadyxxium to produce a durable string to tie up these scrolls, please spirit to the Beechwood Cemetery in Ottawa and gather some from the headstones."

"Yes, sir."

Linnaeus was relieved to be rid Russell. He tried to focus on the list of replantings. It was overwhelming without Kalidasa and Hale. He lay down in an area of the new RD referred to as the crypt, and daydreamed of roaming the countryside in Hammerby, Sweden.

As a mortal, whenever Linnaeus gathered plants and insects he ordinarily experienced a calm exuberance. Sometimes though, he returned home anguished, intimidated by the complexity of life, believing it was beyond classification. One day he came upon the solution—simplify. He selected a soggy horsetail, an aquatic plant, from the huge pile of plant specimens strewn across an old mahogany desk. It had one stamen, which made it easy to classify. And from that point, with a glass of port and a plate of pickled herrings, Linnaeus classified well past sundown. He climbed out of the crypt and returned to the main part of the cave to review the scroll of the American singer.

Lulu Watters was the quintessential blues singer, a tortured soul with a voice of solemnity and anguish. Linnaeus evaluated the case carefully and determined the appropriate placement for Lulu would be as a warbler. "Vireo gilvus," he said, using the binomial nomenclature designation. He travelled to North America and personally conducted the negotiations with The Great Spirit of the Warbler. By the end of the afternoon Lulu was singing in the forests of the Florida panhandle.

Back at the RD, Linnaeus went to work on the souls of the two Tibetan Monks when he heard the unmistakable whir of a materializing 1st Tier. It was Ayodele. "Welcome to the new Replanting Department, Master," said Linnaeus, bowing.

"I want to express my condolences regarding the esteemed Kalidasa and dedicated Hale."

"Thank you, Master."

"I have come to make a special request." Ayodele faced the incomplete Taxonomy of Souls on the wall. "I need your help."

Linnaeus put down the scrolls of the Tibetans monks.

"Cornelius Hoyt failed a reaping."

"Failed?"

"Yes, in the United States, specifically in the state of Maine. I'm afraid he must be disciplined."

"Of course, Master." Linnaeus wanted to pro-tect Cornelius. "Was the mortal integral to The Divine Trajectory of Life?"

"Fortunately—no. Therefore, I have options."

"I would be pleased to have Cornelius back here at the RD, sir."

"Of course, you and he worked together for several hundred years," said Ayodele. "It is for that reason that I had hoped you would have some insight."

"Insight?"

"He disappeared."

"What about Tracking?"

"There is no signal," said Ayodele. "But, I have reason to believe he still exists. Do you have any ideas where he may have gone to hide?"

"No, Master. I'm sorry."

Ayodele nodded pensively. "Do you think he was ever approached by the Traditionalists?"

Despite the concern over the fate of Cornelius, Linnaeus almost smiled. "Master, I find it hard to imagine he would join the Traditionalists."

"These are strange times." Ayodele hovered near the fissure leading out of the cave. "If he contacts you, advise him to go to the ice floe where we had our last cadet meeting."

"Yes, Master."

"Goodbye Linnaeus."

"Goodbye."

Linnaeus moved around the RD, anxious about the welfare of Cornelius, reminded of how he felt when a student was lost on a faraway expedition to collect unknown plants and animals. He also wanted to know how it was possible to evade Tracking, but focused on how to help Cornelius. He was bereft of ideas and returned to the crypt.

As he ruminated, Linnaeus considered visiting a library; he always did his best thinking surrounded by books. He enjoyed fiction at the Stockholm Public Library, learned how to use a computer and surf the internet at the Amsterdam Public Library, reviewed the latest scientific research at the Bod of Oxford. He frequently visited G□ttingen University in Germany to examine with pride an original copy of his 10ᵗʰ Edition of *The Systema Naturae*. Growing restless, he tried to imagine what Sherlock Homes would do. It occurred to Linnaeus that the great detective of Baker Street would start at the Dwelling—the "logical" place to launch an investigation. Although he lamented the untidy state of the new RD, Linnaeus spirited out, and up to the sky.

The sunshine of the Dwelling was a dramatic contrast to Krubera. It was so bright, Linnaeus wanted to build a greenhouse and fill it with Twinflowers. He decided to start his search for clues at the chambers, when Páll came floating across the skerry.

"Hello, Linnaeus, our esteemed RD Manager."

"Greetings," replied Linnaeus warily, aware that Páll was reputed to be an agent of the Traditionalists.

"Might I inquire as to your presence here at the Dwelling?"

"I understand Cornelius may be lost."

"Yes, a pity," said Páll. "We seem to have lost a promising cadet."

"Perhaps, he still exists."

"Possibly, but if necessary, he will be easy to replace."

A container ship carrying truck-sized steel boxes moved past the skerry. The purpose of the immense boat mystified Linnaeus, but he used the distraction to step on a bit of silver residue and ground it down into the snow. It was definitely not endemic to a skerry at the Arctic Circle. He deduced it was the remnants of a scythe, and decided to prevent Páll from finding it and somehow using it against Cornelius.

"What are we to do?" Páll stared out at the ocean. "Our workload expands, but our roster contracts."

Linnaeus was irritated by the flippant remark; it minimized the losses of Kalidasa and Hale.

"The predicament requires leadership," said Páll. "A grand solution! I understand you have a backlog at the RD. It might expedite matters if you revive the old tradition of replanting souls as creatures at the bottom of the food chain."

Linnaeus refused to get embroiled in a debate on the merits of replanting each and every soul individually. "As you say, there is work to be done," he said, looking down and confirming the silver residue was buried. "I will return to the RD."

"Yes, of course," said Páll, walking towards the chambers.

Linnaeus drifted away and rose to the clouds. Over the Baltic Sea, he intuited that Páll, or another Traditionalist, was manipulating Russell. He had observed of late that whenever Russell left the RD to conduct a negotiation with a Great Spirit, he returned late and uncharacteristically argumentative. It was a weak supposition, Linnaeus concluded, but adequate enough to investigate. Somehow it might help Cornelius.

23

In route to Ottawa, Russell rendezvoused with Mortimer at a cottage next to the Crookhaven Lighthouse at the southwestern tip of Ireland.

Russell approached Mortimer and bowed. "May it please your majesty, I have intelligence to report."

Mortimer was disgusted by the obsequious body language of Russell, a drug addict when mortal he retained some of the associated behaviors.

"Sire, I overheard a conversation between Ayodele and Linnaeus."

Mortimer listened attentively. It was an extraordinary development.

"The information will serve you, Sire."

Mortimer was piqued. He wondered if Russell were attempting to use the knowledge he possessed to gain leverage. Mortimer roamed the cottage, turning a corner he stood over the dead lighthouse keepers. He wondered if Russell was shrewd enough to grasp the warning.

"The Master...I mean Ayodele...reported that a cadet failed a reaping," said Russell, staring at the dead men as he explained the crisis regarding Cornelius.

"Excellent. You are destined to stand among the new gentry." In the future, Mortimer would bestow grand titles and dispense with the pedestrian designation of Tier, and scrap primitive tools such as The Book of Expiration Dates, and the Code of Conduct. "What about the Replanting Department?" Mortimer asked.

"It is delinquent in replantings, Sire."

"Very good."

Damaging the RD was a long-term goal of Operation Balghstaf. Mortimer wanted to limit replantings, and thereby forever reduce the overall number of souls. He initially persuaded Russell to betray the RD by requesting that he work undercover "on behalf of the Triumvirate" and gradually coaxed increased duplicity by requesting information on the work of Team Members. The intelligence provided by Russell allowed Páll to locate and kill Sebastian on the west coast of Africa; plans to kill Hale were scrapped when that reaper suffered a lethal accident at an aquarium in California.

"Now, squire, I have something for you." Mortimer carefully handed Russell a microscopic tube constructed of a durable plastic, stolen from a medical research facility. "The vial you hold will require your talent for subterfuge."

"I am at your service, Sire." Russell promptly dropped the tube, causing the normally imperturbable Mortimer to flinch.

"I warn you. Handle it with the utmost caution. Its contents are lethal."

"Yes, Sire."

The tube was as long as a crochet needle, with an infinitesimal diameter. Mortimer pointed to the salt crystals at the bottom, and instructed Russell on how to safely administer droplets of the liquid to a cup of the Universal Elixir, and—if necessary—how to safely unseal the tube and use it against a Grim Reaper.

"Undoubtedly you are wondering what you are expected to do," stated Mortimer. "For now, simply wait. I will contact you when your services are required. Do you understand?"

"Yes, Sire."

The present condition of Nottingham Castle disgusted Mortimer. It had survived wars and sieges over the centuries only to suffer the indignity of its present incarnation as a museum and tourist attraction. It was an abomination.

He sat atop a gate and surveyed the land. A substantial amount of debris littered the surrounding area—homes, shops, roads—all of it to be removed before he could restore the old hunting grounds and forests. Mortimer spirited to the old cave used by the cowardly soldiers loyal to the damnable Edward, and decided he would destroy it when he reconstructed the castle, or fill it with quarrelsome heads-of-state who were unable to adapt to the new world order.

He used a narrow split in the foundation to gain access to a relatively undamaged section of the cellar. He adjusted a painting hanging on a wall, although it had no frame, it was well preserved by the temperature and humidity of the hollow. It was a Rembrandt. Mortimer stole *Storm in the Sea of Galilee* in March of 1990 a museum in Boston. He was in the city to celebrate the Boston Massacre, and to reconnoiter a potential Systematic Multiple Reaping at a sports arena, when an opportunity arose to acquire the painting. During a robbery at the Isabella Stewart Gardner Museum conducted by mortals, Mortimer stole the painting as well as a delicate ancient Chinese vase that he gave to 1st Tier Wu Long of the Great Zone of China.

Mortimer imagined Nottingham Castle restored, standing majestically on the promontory of Castle Rock. He envisioned bejeweled turrets, a tower built with gold, a drawbridge of silver and a gate of ivory. The Great Hall of Nottingham would exceed the opulence of the Hall of Mirrors at Versailles. He would acquire Greek and Egyptian antiquities, and loot the Musée de Louvre for masterpieces by Caron, Bosch, and Delacroix. Most importantly, the throne would be made of sapphire, favorite gemstone of Queen Isabella, past benefactor, confidant and lover.

The dark energy came to Mortimer. *Your kingdom is at hand.*

Mortimer kept two comatose mortals stationed in the United States. They were considered medical mysteries by attending physicians at the extended care facilities, who were unable to diagnose comas induced by a poison from ancient Egypt.

Páll made the discovery of the crucial element at the Cadet Workshop. He was clearing dust off of a sarcophagus when he noticed a unique hieroglyphic of a scarab and a fist. He reported it to Mortimer, explaining that it symbolized the extraordinary power of Medhat. Mortimer complimented Páll on the astute interpretation, but secretly he believed the hieroglyph signified that the *contents* of the sarcophagus held extraordinary power. Mortimer surreptitiously extracted several beetle carcasses, and unsure of what he possessed, experimented on random mortals by using microscopic bits of scarab. But whether it was injected, ingested, or inhaled, it had no impact.

Finally, after many trials, he learned how to use the power of the scarab: a particle of it placed on the aqueous humor of the left eye induced coma, and when a granule was subsequently placed in the right eye it produced an absolutely compliant Grim Reaper. The power of scarab explained how the great Egyptian virtually controlled death in the ancient world—legions of such reapers must have been unstoppable! Mortimer was humbled by the omnipotence of Medhat. He would honor the legendary Grim Reaper by utilizing the scarabs to produce hordes of unquestioning GRs to reconquer the world of the living.

As Operation Balghstaf advanced toward a critical stage, Mortimer traveled to Iowa to retrieve one of the comatose mortals. He arrived in Cedar Falls on a humid day and settled on a billboard that advertised shaving cream. He peeked at the ad and ran his hand over the stubble he had worn for over six hundred years, deciding he would have shaved that fateful morning if he knew he would retain a tired face for centuries.

He found the hospital and put on a custodial uniform in a storage closet on the third floor of the Prairie Medical Center, and emerged with a mop and a bucket—a costume to roam the halls and locate the mortal. A woman wearing blue scrubs promptly stopped Mortimer. "When you have a minute, the toilet overflowed again."

Mortimer was overwhelmed by the sounds of the various medical devices and barely managed to nod. He dragged the bucket and mop to the lavatory and pre-tended to clean, how strange he mused, to behave as an ordinary mortal. Growing impatient, he returned to the storage closet and took the maintenance log to use as a prop. He walked down the hall until he located what he called Drudge 1. He pushed open the door of the suite, and saw the cadaverous Peter Muratov lying on the bed, attached to a multitude of machines.

The walls were covered with pictures of Peter playing college lacrosse, the windowsill was crowded with potted plants, the bed covered with a homemade quilt, and smooth jazz played in the background. Mortimer approached the bed and lifted the tab on a packet containing scarab dust.

"Hello? Excuse me?" A stout woman wearing a beige sweater came out of the bathroom.

Mortimer shook his head as if a language barrier existed, aware of the American amalgam of people and culture.

"Please cover your shoes with the disposable slippers." The woman handed him a box of the paper slippers.

Mortimer assumed the woman was related to Peter based on the similarity of the facial structure.

"Peter, my darling," she said, "how about we read together from my new tablet?"

After Mortimer put on the slippers, he examined the light-bulb in the fixture over the bed and wiped it with a rag. While the woman read *The Huffington Post* out loud, he leaned over Peter and dropped a particle of scarab dust onto the right eye. Mortimer then walked out of the suite and returned to the custodial closet to dump the uniform. As he spirited back to Peter he heard the unmistakable sound of a cardiac monitor flat-lining.

"Peter! Come back!" cried the woman. "I love you, come back!"

The power of the scarab dust humbled Mortimer. He imagined a chapel in the rebuilt Nottingham Castle dedicated to the great Egyptian.

A recorded voice overhead repeated "code blue" and doctors and nurses arrived within seconds to attempt to resuscitate Peter. Mortimer wafted over the team as it worked, marveling at the sophisticated medical techniques. When he was mortal the treatments of the day were brutal. He remembered one leading surgeon, a popular London butcher, applying pigeon dung to lesions and cauterizing wounds with leeches.

Mortimer noticed the soul of Peter gravitating back towards the body, but he guided it away—no miracle today. The doctor instructed the team to back away from the bed. "Let the young man rest in peace."

Mortimer left the hospital with Peter and headed east to Baltimore to execute the next phase of Balghstaf.

24

The Policiá were situated under the trees of an old cemetery on the Isle of the Dead in Port Arthur off Tasmania.

"Any progress, Max?" Ortega asked.

"No Chief," said Officer Maximilian, empowered with extrasensory skills to conduct Tracking. "I have no signal on Kao or Cornelius Hoyt."

Frustrated by the lack of progress locating the rogue cadets, Ortega spirited over to the mainland, flying in and out of the old brick prison of Port Arthur and back to the cemetery. "We have enough work for a whole police force!" he complained, holding up the list:

Cadet Kao AWOL with no signal
Cadet Cornelius Hoyt guilty of a failed reaping (Frank Guerette survived) and AWOL with no signal
3rd Tier Luboslaw and GR-RD/4 Sebastian MIA
Investigating accidental Termination of GR-RD/2 Hale
Monitoring the dubious activities of 1st Tier Mortimer

"Our department will only grow when we successfully prosecute a major case," asserted Ortega. He checked the special pocket of the Policiá cloak for the salt packet, determined to use it at the slightest provocation.

"Chief, how about we contact Master Ayodele regarding the data we have collected on Roger Mortimer?"

"A reasonable proposal Max, but we have to be very careful." These days Chief Ortega avoided contact with Ayodele and the 1st Tiers, unsure of the shifting alliances.

"Wait!" Maximilian held up a hand. "I detect one powerful signal directly north of our present position...ah, I lost it."

"No matter, we have a clue. How far north?"

"Approximately five thousand miles, maybe six."

"Excellent, Max."

They spirited from the isle to Tasmania and landed in Hobart, dressed as mortals and crisscrossed the city seeking a shop that sold maps. The tight, modern suit embarrassed Ortega. He was accustomed to the unrestricting garments of the Hermandades, the original police of medieval Spain. He and Maximilian entered a store and searched a rack of maps, wary of a doddering tourist picking out a postcard. Maximilian chose a booklet, and methodically flipped the pages to a map of eastern Asia. He pointed to a map of Kamchatka. "Chief, I suggest we search this peninsula on the far eastern edge of Russia."

Ortega seized the map, almost knocking over a stack of Violet Crumble. He determined a flight plan to Kamchatka and returned the map to the rack. They hurried down several blocks to a factory with a tall smoke stack emitting steam. Together they ascended with the steam to the clouds. As they gained altitude they shed the suits, which landed on a field during a cricket match to the astonishment of the players.

25

Cornelius sat at the wooden table hewn from the surrounding forest, and examined its construction, impressed by its clean lines. It was a welcomed contrast to the rest of the cheap furnishings of the cabin. "What about meals?" he asked.

"What do you mean?"

"If we're a couple we have to eat. I mean, we have to pretend. There ought to be dirty dishes and some garbage."

"Yes," said Kao, "of course."

"You'll have to do the cooking."

"Why?"

"You're a woman."

"If we have to pose as a couple, you will have to get your head out of the seventeenth century!"

"But..."

"Men cook. Men clean. Men..."

"Okay, okay." He went to the cabinet over the sink and removed several cans of chicken noodle soup.

"Unacceptable."

"Do I have to open the cans, too?"

"No." Kao smiled. "I am...I was...a vegetarian."

Cornelius laughed, aware of vegetarianism from conversations with Linnaeus. He went over to the wood-burning stove and lit it with a match. "Kao, can I ask you a personal question."

"Yes."

Cornelius placed two glasses of water on the table and sat down. "How were you recruited?"

"It may surprise you." Kao struggled to open a can of beans with a can opener. "I fell and broke my neck."

"What happened?"

"It was the 1970s, and I was a feminist," Kao explained. "While I was giving a speech..."

"What's a feminist?"

"Basically, it is a person who advocates for equal rights for women." Kao passionately explained how it included political, economic and social rights. "The majority of people, including most women, were against us, in fact, we were portrayed as radicals. We argued for fundamental changes to our culture, including the liberation of sex."

Cornelius looked down. "Um, so what happened?"

"I was standing on the scaffolding of a temporary stage and it collapsed. I fell and severely injured my spinal cord." Kao separated strands of hair in the back of her head to reveal a scar.

"You mentioned it would surprise me," said Cornelius; he could listen to her voice for hours. "Lots of people die from accidents."

"The surprising part is I was visited at the hospital by a Grim Reaper."

"You were *visited*?" The disclosure stunned Cornelius. "You were alive?"

"Yes, I mean, I was unconscious." Kao lit the lantern. "Anyway, as I lay dying, the reaper explained that I had a chance to help women. I remember thinking I must be dreaming of the mythological Shinigami, but it was so *real*." Kao smelled the beans and pushed away the can. "The reaper explained how women traditionally received a disproportionate number of Excruciating Deaths."

"Who was the Grim Reaper?"

"2nd Tier Luboslaw...our contact."

"Okay, but how exactly would a female Grim Reaper help mortal women?"

"Provocateurs believe the presence of female reapers will balance assignments, and consequently reduce Excruciating Deaths applied to women."

Cornelius was sympathetic and wondered if he ruined the plan when he went back to Mount Fuji and set in motion the problems that caused them to seek refuge.

"It was kind of you to inquire," said Kao. She moved to the window to observe a rising thunderstorm.

Cornelius picked up the bowls and washed the dishes at the sink. At the sound of trees crashing, he went to the window and pointed to a plume of smoke. "A lightning strike," he said, excited. "C'mon, let's go take a look."

He ran out to the woods, pushing past tree branches and climbing over boulders and came to a clearing scorched down to the dirt, blackened and smoldering under the heavy rain. Kao caught up and walked purposefully, as if conducting an investigation.

"Strange lightning strike," said Cornelius. He touched the scorched ground. It was cold. When he climbed up onto a beehive-shaped rock and saw that it had an unnatural symmetry, he thought of Linnaeus, who regularly talked about strange natural phenomena.

Kao approached the rock, and turned abruptly and ran back toward the cabin.

"Wait!" Cornelius caught up to her at the cabin. "What's wrong?"

"The rock had an image of an anchor and flag."

Cornelius laughed nervously. "The ashes probably just hit it a certain way."

"No, it was drawn," insisted Kao. "Luboslaw was trying to warn us."

"I don't understand."

"The anchor and flag was a symbol of the Polish underground during World War II," said Kao, packing bottles of argan oil into a hemp bag.

"I'm sorry, but exactly what does it mean?" He was afraid of the answer.

"It means Luboslaw came to Kamchatka to contact us, but he only had enough time to draw the symbol."

Cornelius was petrified, only moments ago a reaper had destroyed Luboslaw just a few hundred feet from the cabin.

"The rain diluted the oil!" Kao opened a bottle of argan and hastily poured it over Cornelius.

He emptied a bottle over Kao.

Thunder bullied the steel cabin.

"I have an idea," said Kao, handing the hemp bag filled with bottles of oil to Cornelius. "We will go to Australia."

"Australia? How about Krubera?"

Kao stuffed her notepad into another bag. "We will only endanger Linnaeus."

"I guess you're right."

"I have a friend—Woggan, he will know what to do." Kao headed out. Cornelius surveyed the cabin, gazing at the bed. He joined Kao outside, and together they spirited south.

26

The red-bricked Old Baltimore Shot Tower was a historical landmark. Mortimer remembered the windswept day when the austere Charles Carroll of Carrollton, last surviving signatory of the Declaration of Independence, laid the cornerstone. Earlier on that drizzly morning, Mortimer had reaped the architect Thaddeus Chase as he fornicated with a slave. At 234¼ feet, the tower was the tallest structure in the United States when completed in 1828. It had always relaxed Mortimer to scrutinize the process as workers dropped molten lead from the platform and it gathered speed travelling down the tower, hit a sieve and splashed down to a vat of cold water, emerging as shot for pistols, rifles, and cannons. These days Mortimer used the Tower as a landmark. He cruised over Baltimore and landed on the platform of the tower and ordered Peter, aka Drudge 1, to sit and wait.

Mortimer went uptown and donned a pair of jeans and a denim shirt from a line of laundry and materialized in an alley. He walked down East Baltimore Street past the Hustler Club and entered an electronics store. He observed several transactions, wondering if the tongue and nose piercings on the salesman were a form of punishment. He purchased two cell phones and returned to the shot tower, patting Peter on the head.

Using one cell phone, Mortimer dialed the White House. He told the operator of an impending train disaster and claimed responsibility on behalf of the Saudi Arabian Liberation Army. He hoped to complicate Middle East alliances, already severely tested by the recent bombing of Revolution Tower in Tehran by Great Britain in retaliation for the "murder" of Ambassador Lockhart. Mortimer flinched when the cell phone unexpectedly rang, playing the melody of "We Will Rock You." He dumped it down the gullet of the tower and escorted Peter to the Stern Avenue Tunnel.

The sight of Peter standing on the track caused the engineer of the CXT locomotive to hit the air breaks. Strained by the stress of its tonnage, the freight train derailed and a tank of flammable tripropylene ruptured and exploded (aided by a match struck by Mortimer). Heavy smoke of toxic chlorine poured out of the Stern Avenue Tunnel—an exhaust pipe from hell, and as expected, destroyed Peter. The heat melted the old blue frieze over the entrance of the tunnel and caused the century-old pipes to disintegrate, leading to a precipitous decline in the available water to fight the blaze.

State and federal agencies mobilized. Mortimer stingily granted that Baltimore firefighters were courageous, but as he drifted over the area he exulted at the chaos. It was just the beginning. If Balghstaf were a swordfight, the derailed locomotive was only a cut. The kill was to come.

Mortimer infiltrated the White House using the original fireplace of the State Dining Room, and moved down the halls, unimpressed by the presidential portraits. He arrived at the Oval Office, bemused to find President Carson posing with a troupe of Boy Scouts. The national security advisor and CIA director cut short the meeting with the scouts to give the president a briefing about the disaster in Baltimore. Mortimer sat on the mantelpiece to eavesdrop; fascinated by the complexities of the crisis he had created.

A tall man with glasses updated the president on the claims made by a previously unidentified terrorist group regarding the train derailment. "How do you want to respond Madam President?" he asked.

"I want confirmation on these terrorists," ordered Carson, lighting a cigarette. "And I want actionable intelligence."

"Rose, we have to release a statement," suggested an older, overweight man.

"Of course, Samuel, please draft one." President Carson put out the cigarette, and popped a Nicorette lozenge.

As the president verbalized ideas about a statement, Mortimer exited the White House, pleased by the status of the catastrophe.

When he reached the Sandia Mountains of New Mexico, Mortimer flew in the vicinity of an eagle, and understood why the United States had selected the majestic bird as its emblem. The clear air made it an easy spirit, when suddenly a strange group of bulbous creatures rose simultaneously from the ground. He moved towards the edge of the atmosphere to avoid a mammoth blue lizard, but when a ridiculous Hello Kitty floated up, he realized they were only hot air balloons. As hundreds of balloons ascended, he cursed the crowded sky and the camera-toting mortals.

He approached Albuquerque Hospital to retrieve Drudge 2. Matthew Blaine loved Harley-Davidsons, and worked with the local police to demonstrate motorcycle safety. So it came as a surprise last year when he crashed on Route 85. The police labeled it an accident, unaware it was caused by the appearance of a Grim Reaper on the handlebars, and doctors were similarly unaware that the coma was induced by scarab dust.

Mortimer landed on a fire escape off Central Avenue Southwest and climbed down to the sidewalk. He walked towards a church spire and entered the nearby rectory. It was quaint, decorated in a Victorian style, with sumptuous chairs and carpets, dark woods and two stained glass windows. Mortimer valued the solitude—a quality he expected to lose as king, and wondered if it would be possible to build a sanctuary on a grand scale. He imagined Bryce Canyon Castle or the Grand Canyon Manor House, and that one day he would tell a roundtable of noble Grim Reapers a riotous tale of how he play-acted as a priest during Operation Balghstaf. He quickly gathered clergy apparel and went to the Albuquerque Hospital.

Flummoxed by the revolving doors of hospital, Mortimer paused before walking over to the reception desk. He was greeted by an elderly woman. "Can I help you, Reverend?"

"Yes please, the location of Matthew Blaine." He neglected to adequately cover the rope scars from the ancient hanging, but the woman remained focused on the computer screen.

"Room 220," she said. "Have a nice day."

Mortimer took the stairs, fearful of encountering mortals on an elevator and risking conversation.

After he collected Drudge 2, Mortimer spirited to Las Vegas. He last experienced the city on July 26, 1969 on a trip to complete several assignments, and observed the opening show of Elvis; he enjoyed the music, but was irritated that the singer was called "the King."

He parked Matthew on the top of the Bellagio and followed a pair of mustachioed drunkards to The Mirage. The two passed out and Mortimer stole a pair of pants, a shirt, and a wad of cash. He found the casino, its energy was irresistible. He vowed that when reapers inhabited the world unrestrained, Monte Carlo would serve as a reaper playground, while he would use trips to Las Vegas as rewards for valuable mortals. Mortimer exchanged the cash for chips and approached a roulette wheel, a game he had played many times. He promptly lost all the money on two bets.

He walked out of The Mirage, and dematerialized in an alley to contemplate an appropriate retaliation. When a prostitute and a john crept down the alley to conduct business, Mortimer returned to the hotel, spiriting past the artificial volcano. Although eager to get to Mexico, he hovered over the roulette wheel and watched one gambler flirt with a waitress and a security guard escort an inebriated woman away from the table. As the roulette came to stop, Mortimer gracefully tipped the ball, causing it to stop on a number corresponding to a bet. He created six consecutive winners before a pit boss shut down the game.

Mexico proudly celebrated the completion of the Puebla Nuclear Power Plant with a parade filled with floats and marching bands. The festivities inundated the city of Puebla with visitors and filled the jails with inebriated revelers—most charged with disorderly conduct and released within twelve hours as a good will gesture. As the latest boiling-water reactor, the Puebla Nuclear Power Plant was advertised as the safest in the world.

Mortimer spirited to the city of Puebla with Drudge 2 in tow, and coasted to the reactor. The byzantine switches and dials of the control room, and a conversation among a small group of engineers, demoralized Mortimer. *It is easy to destroy*, reassured dark energy.

Mortimer positioned Matthew Blaine next to a set of levers marked EMERGENCIA REFRIGANTE DEL REACTOR holding a plastic vial of chlorine trifluride, and instructed him to pour the fluid over the control board. Mortimer rapidly fled the nuclear power plant and headed to Mexico City. He landed atop the headquarters of Televisa on Avenida Vasco de Quiroga and used a cell phone to call with news of an accident at the nuclear power plant in Puebla. He placed a second call to the newspaper *Reforma* about an inexplicable increase in radiation levels around Puebla. Finally, he placed a call to radio station 104.1 and reported that women and children in the vicinity of the Puebla Nuclear Power Plant were collapsing, and that the army had quarantined the city.

Mortimer was pleased by subsequent reports of the mandatory evacuation of the power plant. Although emergency safety protocol was followed and the nuclear reactor shut down without a radiation leak, citizens accustomed to a corrupt local government doubted its reassurances. By sunset, President Delgado had ordered the military to stand on high alert and instituted several security measures, including a national curfew.

Surprisingly, Matthew survived the incident, but Mortimer still feared the potential for lingering effects of radiation on a GR body and dropped Drudge 2 into the Gulf of Mexico. Next, Mortimer traveled south toward Belize in order to avoid Florida, lest he encounter a Provocateur guarding Cape Canaveral, and from Central America he turned northeast on course to Nottingham Castle, satisfied by the chaos he had sown.

27

Thirty three days atop an Illawarra flame tree battling a monsoon of Residual Images exhausted Woggan. Awakening, he was restored by the sounds of the Pacific and the sight of the coast. A day of sunbeams. He tightened the bark fibers that kept the scythe tied to the tree; as an Observer he had no obligation to lug it around. He pushed back a head of wild black hair and smiled, revealing radiant teeth undamaged by refined sugar. He sat in the tree among a cluster of red bell flowers and waited. Termination was coming.

In the 5th century, Woggan was a seventeen year-old Australian, gifted at building canoes from the bark of the eucalyptus. He had belonged to the Birrabirragal clan living on the rocky shores of Djubuguli as part of an extended family. They lived as aboriginals had for millennia, fishing in the cove, hunting kangaroos and wallabies, and spending evenings huddled in the caves creating art.

When ripped away from the tribe to be a Grim Reaper, Woggan was assigned the role of Observer. For hundreds and hundreds of years he produced scrolls on the cultures, geography, and climate of Oceania, a region that roughly included the Marianna Islands to Hawaii, southeast to Easter Island, and on to Kiribati.

The last assignment, over two hundred twenty five years ago, scarred Woggan.

When ordered to conduct reconnaissance on Australia, he begged to be reassigned, but undeveloped zones were dwindling and the request was denied. Past deaths in Australia were by natural causes, accidents, euthanasia, or abortion, and Woggan understood the arrival of reaperkind would destroy the aboriginal way of life. As ordered, he conducted the reconnaissance, but he submitted skewed reports, producing scrolls that indicated the continent lacked value to Grim Reapers. Sadly, the reports were made obsolete in 1788 when Captain Phillip and the crew of the HMS *Sirius* made landfall on a beach of Burrowaree and put up a crude lighthouse. As the colony grew, Woggan observed the warped culture of the guards and convicts, and hoped the colony might collapse and The Society of Death would abandon Australia. When the colony flourished, and led to establishment of the Zone of Australia, Woggan learned to cry the dry tears of a Grim Reaper.

When mortal, he lived within the rains and rivers and sunshine and ocean. As a reaper he lamented the separation from nature he experienced. Although he saw the whole of Australia as a reaper, and learned to appreciate its infinite beauty, it was no consolation. He had existed long enough to witness the slaughter of fathers and mothers, boys and girls, and the grotesque changes to Burrowaree. He longed to hurt The Society of Death.

Woggan headed down Hickson Road in Sydney wearing blue jeans and a sweatshirt with slanted lines in front, a traditional Aboriginal symbol for rain, and carried a pocketful of $2 coins with the image of an aborigine elder. Woggan was stimulated by the kinetic city, while at the same time possessed by a desire to agitate the world of the living.

He came upon the historic district, and stopped at the bay window of the Prison Hulk Café, amazed by its immense fish tank filled with cardinal fish, dotty backs, gobies, and tangs. A mystical impulse urged Woggan to talk to the man coming out of the café and downing a pint of beer.

"Are you the artist?" Woggan pointed to the opals displayed in the window.

"Technically a lapidarist, artist sounds a bit high-class for me," said the man, peering out at Woolloomooloo. "Come in, I'll show you a few of my rocks."

The mortal handed Woggan an opal—round and radiant, blue and green and violet. It transported him to the waves, wide open spaces and birds. "This is so beautiful."

"Thank you, mate." Flanagan handed a business card to Woggan. "Do you have access to the web?"

"A web?"

Flanagan pointed to an ad on a table with a brief explanation on how the jewelry came from black opals mined from Lightning Ridge. The table held pendants, droplets, and brooches, and pictures of bracelets, rings, and bangles. Woggan gestured to a triangular opal. "A tiny boomerang?"

Flanagan laughed, and combed his untamed beard with his fingers. He handed Woggan the triangular opal. "Here, hold it up to the sunlight."

"What a wonderful stone!" Woggan felt strange, volatile—the stone made him feel alive. "I imagine the harbor wild, without steel and cement and streets and buildings and boats and bridges."

"You're a poet." Flanagan cut an apple with a paring knife.

Woggan reflected on the clan elders, authentic poets of folklore, lost during the dark period. He was sad, angry. Alive and dead. Awake but dreaming. "No," he blurted. "I am a Grim Reaper."

"'Scuse me?"

"Grim Reaper!" Woggan swung an imaginary scythe.

"You're a farmer?" Flanagan asked.

"No!" Woggan wanted to challenge the mortal. "I am a Grim Reaper!"

Flanagan removed a toothpick from a pocket and picked out a seed from a molar. "Ah, mate, how 'bout a short black to sober you up?"

"I want you to understand." Woggan snatched the paring knife by the blade and squeezed it without injury. Flanagan went ashen.

"Now do you believe me?" Woggan asked.

Flanagan nodded rapidly.

Woggan picked up the round opal. "I want to buy the ocean rock." He counted out twenty coins and piled $40 on the table.

"Its $280," said Flanagan, fumbling a pack of cigarettes.

"A rock...or your soul?"

"How about you just take it?"

"I want to pay." Woggan gestured to the pile of coins.

"Okay." Flanagan wiped away a drop of spittle.

"My name is Woggan."

"Okay."

"Opal Man?"

"Yeah?"

"Are you afraid?"

"Yeah."

Woggan smiled.

28

Ortega and Maximilian cruised over the Kamchatka peninsula, up its eastern coast on the Pacific Ocean and down the western coast on the Okhotsk Sea. Ortega was overwhelmed by the vast expanse of wilderness, and wanted to call off the search for Kao and Cornelius; privately, he doubted that the two fugitives still existed. Ortega had learned that Roger Mortimer frequented Crumpets espresso bar on Craven Street in London at noon on weekdays—highly suspicious behavior for a 1st Tier—and he wanted to conduct surveillance on the 1st Tier.

They landed invisibly on a street in the city of Petropavlovsk-Kamchatski. "How are we expected to search such an immense area ourselves?" Ortega asked.

"I swear I detected a signal," countered Maximilian, defensively.

Ortega admired the gold onion domes of the Temple of the Sacred Trinity, as he considered an alternative plan. "Max, I have a somewhat unfair request to make."

"Sir?"

"You will have to continue the search alone."

Maximilian stood tall. "As you command."

Ortega appreciated of the loyalty and dedication of Maximilian. "I recommend you limit your search to significant natural formations."

"I will start by searching the area around each volcano."

"A daunting task, I counted over two hundred." It frustrated Ortega to leave Maximilian in Kamchatka when they were on the verge of apprehending Mortimer. "These cadets are desperate, and cunning enough to have dodged Tracking. Are you prepared to use force?"

Maximilian presented two salt packets.

"You will commit six days...precisely." Ortega peered up to the sky. "We'll rendezvous in one hundred and forty four hours at Trafalgar Square."

"London?"

"Affirmative, Max."

"Yes, sir!"

29

They landed on the escarpment as if ill-paired ballet dancers, Kao performing a grand jeté with legs elegantly split before touching down, while Cornelius clumsily executed a tombé and hit the ground hard, exhausted by a typhoon over the Philippine Sea. They removed the heavy clothing from Kamchatka, and as he reapplied argan oil, Cornelius noticed that the holes in his shoulder and Achilles were gone and the skin smooth.

"Just as I remember it." Kao twirled with arms outstretched, as if a captive animal released to the wild.

When Cornelius lived, the existence of a southern continent was only a myth. While at the RD he learned about Australia from Linnaeus, and often imagined living as a deck hand aboard the *Endeavor* on an Allowance to Act Mortal. He had admired James Cook and always felt it was unfair that he suffered an Excruciating Death in Hawaii.

"Woggan lives in these mountains," said Kao.

"Are we going to spirit or walk?"

"I say we walk."

Cornelius agreed, excited to walk on rough terrain. He listened to the birds singing and gazed out at the panorama of cliffs and forests. "What does your friend do?" he asked.

"He was an Observer." Kao knelt to examine the trunk of a red cedar tree as the terrain transitioned to bush and woodland. "In the past, Observers conducted reconnaissance in unfamiliar territories. They became obsolete when there were no new territories to explore."

"How will he help us survive?"

"I trust that he will be able to help us."

"All right, but how are we supposed to find him?"

"By getting lost." Kao smiled at a butterfly with turquoise wings. "I know it sounds strange."

Impulsively, Cornelius kissed Kao. It was sweet and special, exhilarating and calming. Her lips were so moist. He was unsure what to expect, and overjoyed when Kao smiled. As they walked up a trail on Mount Keira, holding hands amidst the lush foliage, Cornelius experienced a transformation—he was hungry. Was it real? And what about Kao? Maybe it was her long hair, held up with a string fashioned out of the fibrous bark of a eucalyptus tree, or maybe it was walking with a natural gait, but she was spectacular, almost intimidating—beautiful and intelligent, with an intangible power beyond a Grim Reaper. Cornelius was exhilarated and wanted to spirit around the world. Distracted, he tripped over a tree root and fell.

"Are you all right?" Kao gently touched his scraped palms. "You're bleeding!"

He examined the cut. It was irrefutable. He was alive! And Kao? "Are you sweating?" he asked, almost pleading for it be true.

Kao smelled her armpits and grimaced. "What does it mean?"

Cornelius hesitated to say, it might break the spell.

"We have changed," said Kao, running a hand over stubbly legs. "How could it have happened?"

"I don't know."

"Are we sick?"

"It means we're alive!"

Kao narrowed her eyes and bit her lower lip.

"It's a miracle, right?"

"Yes, of course," said Kao, seemingly preoccupied.

"What's wrong?"

"I cannot help but wonder if we are now in *more* danger." Kao checked her pulse, and quickly removed her hand from her wrist as if removing it from a hot stove.

Cornelius was crestfallen. A second ago he was excited to be free, with a chance to live again. But Kao was right, they were a grave threat to The Society of Death, and had no way of defending themselves. Tears welled-up and he turned away, beleaguered by mix of hazards and dreams. "At least we can stop covering ourselves with argan oil."

"Yes." Kao kissed Cornelius. "And you are right, it is a miracle."

Cornelius savored the moment, even if it lasted only a few minutes and he was struck dead again. They chased one another and collapsed to the ground, breathing gulps of fresh air. Kao snuggled up to Cornelius. He wanted to find a bed and lay together under the blankets.

Kao sighed heavily.

He was at the edge of sleep, listening to Kao breathe, aware of the warmth of the sunshine and the breeze and the chirping birds. Paradise.

Kao got up and brushed bits of grass from her clothes, scanning the horizon. He sat up, disappointed the moment was gone.

"What has made us change?" Kao wiped sweat from her face. "Maybe it is something about Australia?"

"I started to feel different on Mount Fuji."

"Yes, in hindsight, I had a symptom of this...this change...when I was unable to hear the mountain climbers around my chamber. As a child I lost some hearing in my left ear," she explained, placing a finger over the opening of her right ear to test the left. "As a reaper my auditory sense was perfect." Kao gazed at Cornelius. "The only explanation appears to be our relationship."

Cornelius blushed. He wondered if marriage would be appropriate when a man with dark skin and a wide grin pushed past a few trees and emerged out of the bush.

"Who are you?" Cornelius demanded, frightened. "What do you want?"

Kao hugged the man. "Woggan!"

Cornelius shuffled awkwardly. "Pleased to make your acquaintance," he said, reverting to etiquette learned back in Natick, but he was angered by the intrusion.

Woggan gestured to the trail. "Are you enjoying Mount Keira?"

"Yes, the mountain is as lovely as ever," said Kao. "My friend, we have come...how do I explain all that has transpired?"

"No need," responded Woggan, he seemed to grasp the whole situation—the lost scythes, the argan oil, the inexplicable physical changes. "If it's all right, I'd like to join you on your trek across the mountain?"

"Please do!"

"No, wait," Cornelius insisted. "What's the plan?"

"We have to have patience," said Kao, guiding Cornelius to a spot with a view past the trees and pointed to the bright sun.

Woggan darted to a eucalyptus tree and picked a white flower and handed it to Kao.

"Don't you understand?" Cornelius was exasperated. "We're guilty of several violations, and we've changed... we're alive!"

Woggan squinted. "Do I detect an accent?"

"Excuse me?" Cornelius was dumbfounded; unaware he sounded similar to the English sailors and Irish convicts of the late 18th century colonization of Sydney.

"Are we on a tight schedule...captain?" asked Woggan with an exaggerated salute.

"What the hell?" Cornelius moved aggressively toward Woggan, who merely floated to the top of a huge boulder.

"Stop it, both of you," shouted Kao. "We have to work together!"

Cornelius resented the warmth Kao felt toward the Observer.

Woggan pulled out a small, curved object from his belt and headed down a trail.

Cornelius resisted an urge to fight, it was no use, and he was frightened of the weapon Woggan held. Kao pleaded for them to cooperate. Woggan turned and gently offered the weapon to Cornelius. A peaceful gesture.

Cornelius accepted it warily, and admired the skill it required to carve. "Incredible, from what animal did you get the bone?"

"Kangaroo."

Cornelius was ignorant of kangaroos. "It's a weapon, right?"

"Sometimes we used it to attack a man, how do you say? Hand-to-hand combat, but mostly to hunt."

"How?"

"You hurl it at the target." Woggan held out the boomerang. "This is a throwstick, but others you throw and it returns to you."

"Really?" Cornelius was skeptical.

"I will show you one day."

Kao sighed loudly. "I wonder whether a boomerang will protect us from the wrath of a 1st Tier."

Woggan smiled. "Boomerangs were not designed to fight Grim Reapers."

Cornelius became dizzy and sat on the ground, unsure of the extent of the transformation he wondered if the changes were stable.

"Is something wrong?" Kao asked.

Woggan came over to Cornelius. "When did you last eat?"

"You mean food?"

"Yes, food," said Woggan, laughing.

"Oh, about three hundred fifty years ago."

"We have to get you both something," said Woggan. "I suggest we go to the city, you'll be safer among mortals and we can get food." He pointed to a trail leading out of the escarpment to the city of Woollongong. "Are you able to walk?"

"Yes, I'm okay," said Cornelius.

Kao stopped Woggan. "Do you understand what has happened to us?"

"I have no expertise on reapers changing to mortals." Woggan resumed hiking.

"Tell us what you believe," begged Cornelius, urgent and anxious, unsure if he and Kao were only being tormented with a taste of life as a prelude to Expulsion.

"I've heard stories of reapers who undergo a meta... meta..."

"Metamorphosis?" interjected Kao. "What stories?"

"Dreamtime tells us love changes rocks to food and clouds to flowers."

"Dreamtime?" The jumble of words confused Cornelius.

Kao kissed Cornelius. "He means our love transformed us." Although he was embarrassed to blush, the kiss was sumptuous.

"Dreamtime says a soul flourishes with love," said Woggan, smiling. "Now, I suggest we keep moving."

They hiked to the plateau of Mount Keira, and then headed downhill past an old World War II battery surrounded by high weeds. The sight of the ocean made Cornelius run down the hill and across the highway to the beach. He filled his lungs with a deep breath. He had seen the Pacific Ocean strictly from high altitudes; up close the waves were magnificent. It was intoxicating. He wanted to swim and bolted toward the water.

"Stop!" screamed Kao, pointing to the lighting in the eastern part of the horizon. "If we can survive saltwater, it means we can be harmed by lightning." Cornelius stopped, and retreated as a wave raced up the beach.

They walked along the shoulder of Mount Keira Road, and came to McCabe Park in the residential part of the city. "You two wait, I will return with help," assured Woggan. "It may take all day, but I will return."

"Where are you going?" Kao asked. "Have you made contact with a mortal? I mean, apart from us."

"I observed a friend."

"A friend?" Cornelius was impressed.

"Yes." Woggan waved casually and walked down Crown Street.

30

At a quiet beach, Woggan gazed up at a paraglider approaching from the west, charmed by the emerald wings of the tiny aircraft and the blue helmet and orange windbreaker of the woman. He imagined it was a lorakeet with the face of a human. The woman made a soft landing, stripped down to a bikini and jumped in the ocean for a swim. He wanted to stay, but he had promise to help Kao.

At the Hulk Prison Café, Woggan saw Flanagan positioning an easel on the sidewalk with a poster about the upcoming Sydney Jewelry Show.

"Flanagan?" Woggan smelled the familiar scent of rum.

"Hi again, um...how are you?"

Woggan was relieved, contacting a mortal risked an awful Expulsion, but the choice of Flanagan was inspired. The imposing man seemed warm and unguarded. Woggan especially appreciated the way he treated opals as gifts from the natural world to be handled as sacred totems.

"It's a fine day, mate." Flanagan shut his eyes tight and faced the sun.

"Yes it is."

"Do you want to walk?" Flanagan asked. "This probably isn't the best place for us to talk."

"Walking?" Woggan hesitated. It would be calamitous if he somehow blundered and frightened the man away.

"Yeah, walking." Flanagan sneezed. "You do walk?"

"Walking, okay." Woggan was anxious to get back to Kao and Cornelius.

"Darling!" called Flanagan. Carolyn, the owner of the café sat at the bar, organizing a pile of receipts.

"Yeah, Slim?" Woggan was confused, Flanagan was heavyset.

"Will you keep an eyeball on the pebbles?"

"No problem, honey."

Flanagan suggested they head south. As they walked, Woggan window-shopped, intrigued by displays of cutlery, cigars, and surfboards, and amused by a dog groomer at work on a poodle.

"Anyway, why...you know, why *me*?"

"I contacted you because of the opals."

"Fair enough." Flanagan walked to a vendor and ordered a cup of espresso.

Woggan was unaccustomed to conversation. "Ah, how are the opals?"

"Always a joy." Flanagan tasted the espresso and frowned. He tripped over a crack but caught hold of a lamppost.

"Are you okay?" Woggan had witnessed the ruinous impact of alcohol on aboriginals and had second-thoughts about contacting Flanagan.

"I'm swell, Mr. Reaper."

"Woggan."

"Okay, mate. Woggan."

They walked to a park, and Flanagan sat on a bench, belched, and lit a cigarette. "So, tell me about death?"

"I have no responsibility to reap."

"I mean, what happens, you know...when you cark it? C'mon, give me some inside information."

"Life terminates."

"Yeah, mate, but what *happens*?"

"Most souls are replanted," explained Woggan.

"You mean reincarnated?"

Woggan shrugged.

"What do you do?"

"Observe."

"Observe what?" Flanagan exhaled smoke and coughed.

"The world of the living." Woggan explained how he was recruited as a Grim Reaper because he survived a walkabout during a severe drought by relying on his exceptional skills of observation. "Observers were deployed to prepare new areas for reapers."

Flanagan whined about having a headache. "New areas?"

"I belonged to the Birrabirragal clan of Burrowaree, and you Europeans, you brought illness and Grim Reapers to our sacred home." He stared at the flowers of a bush.

Flanagan put out the cigarette. "Um, do you want to do something?"

"Yes." Woggan looked out at the cove. "I want to experience the ocean."

"Hmm, you want the ocean. Oh, I know, how about a ferry ride?"

"Will I be safe?" Woggan made it clear that saltwater was dangerous for reapers.

"You'll be safe."

"What about your opals?"

"Right." Flanagan called Carolyn at the café and requested she lock up the opals.

"You trust your friend?"

"Of course, we live together," explained Flanagan. "Wait here, I'll get us tickets." He headed over to a wharf, busy with the arrivals and departures of ferries, and returned with two tickets. They boarded a ferry and sat on the top-deck to protect against a random spray of saltwater. It was a pleasant ride, except when Flanagan rushed to the bathroom to vomit.

At Oceanworld aquarium, Woggan paused at the door.

"Come on, you have to have faith." Flanagan led Woggan toward the Shark Tunnel. "I promise you'll stay dry."

The proximity of the saltwater in the aquarium terrified Woggan, but he relaxed when he noticed children giggling.

"How do you like it Woggan?"

"It's fantastic," he whispered, absorbed by the underwater world of turtles, octopuses, and giant stingrays. He envied the diver swimming among the sea life, until he saw a shark. "Watch out!" he shouted.

Flanagan put an arm around Woggan. "The sharks are Grey Nurse."

"Do they bite?" he asked, pointing to the spear-tipped teeth.

"Yeah, but only crabs and squid."

Woggan turned to Flanagan. "Thank you. I wanted the ocean and you found a way."

"You're welcome, mate."

Woggan and Flanagan returned to the wharf, and walked leisurely back to the Prison Hulk Café. It was late. The neighborhood was quiet except for a couple strolling past the pansies, roses, and geranium flowing out of the hanging baskets, ceramic pots, and small gardens along Circular Quay West.

"Okay, Woggan," said Flanagan, yawning. "Do you want something to eat?"

"I don't eat."

"Right, I forgot." Flanagan stepped into the café, and unlocked the safe, picking up the bag of opals. "I have the

Emporium gig over the weekend...rich people," he mumbled, conspiratorially. He removed a carton of milk from the refrigerator and drank straight from the container.

Carolyn emerged from the back of the café and insisted that he use a glass.

"Okay, darling," said Flanagan, putting away the milk. "C'mon, Woggan, let's go." They walked down to a convenience store and Flanagan purchased a pack of cigarettes, and Woggan brought two containers of cut fruit—watermelon wedges and papaya, and two bottled waters—with the last of his $2 coins.

"I want to express my gratitude," said Woggan. "I saw the ocean. I hope it fills my Residual Images."

"Residual what?"

"Dreams," said Woggan, apologetically.

"Hey, how 'bout I get an opal in its natural state and together we make it a gem."

"I would be honored."

Suddenly, a man snatched the bag of opals from Flanagan. The assailant sprinted across the street and hopped over a guardrail. Flanagan ran a few yards, but he was hobbled by arthritic knees, and the man got away. When Flanagan returned to the sidewalk, Woggan was holding the bag. "What the hell?" Flanagan accepted the bag, opened it and counted the opals.

Woggan was jubilant. He had used reaper powers to *help* a mortal by spiriting into position to confront the thief and demanding the return of the opals. When the thief responded with a racial slur, Woggan hovered upward, causing the man to drop the bag and run.

"Thank you," said Flanagan. "You didn't…"

"No, he's still alive."

"Oh, okay." Flanagan held up the bag of opals. "These are valuable. I owe you."

Woggan smiled wide.

"Wait, let me guess." Flanagan laughed. "You already want something."

"I have two friends, they're…it's hard to explain. Anyway, they need help."

"They're your friends? Are they…I can't believe I'm saying this…are they alive?"

"Yes."

"All right, mate, anything at all" said Flanagan. "What do they need?"

"Everything."

"Everything!" Flanagan laughed. "Okay, so you mean cash and identification?"

Woggan had only considered food and clothing. "Yes, cash," he said, "but, what do you mean…identification?"

"You're friends have nothing?"

"That's right."

"They'll have to have some form of identification…you know, a driver's license, or at least a photo card, maybe a passport."

"You can get these things?" Woggan asked.

"Yeah, for a price..."

"They have no way to pay."

"I'll handle it," said Flanagan, biting a fingernail. "It's all right, I know some people." He held up the bag of opals. "Besides, I owe you."

Woggan returned to McCabe Park and found Kao and Cornelius asleep on the grass. He gently roused the exhausted pair, offering the water and the cups of fruit. They were gluttonous, slurping and laughing, spitting watermelon seeds. Cornelius almost consumed the rind, and Kao gave up trying to stay clean, letting the juices flow down her hands and wrists. After gorging, they ran to the public toilets.

When they returned, Cornelius lay back down on the park lawn. An unsteady and pale Kao sat down gingerly. "I feel sick," she said. "Please, we have to get toothbrushes and I need...personal items."

"I will introduce you to Flanagan."

"The mortal?" Cornelius asked. The word felt strange now that he was "mortal" again.

"Yes." Woggan held up the cell phone belonging to Flanagan, and as instructed, used it to get headshots, explaining it was important in order to get identification.

"Where does your friend live?" Cornelius asked, rubbing his eyes due to the afterimage of the flash of the digital camera.

"He will be at the Prison Hulk at 9 a.m. Monday."

"Prison Hulk?" Cornelius laughed. "Your friend is in jail?"

"No, it's a place...a restaurant." Woggan smiled, and suggested Kao and Cornelius rest a bit longer while he returned the cell phone to Flanagan.

31

Mortimer frantically paced in a subterranean hollow. It was a quarter-mile south of Nottingham Castle, and only recently discovered, but unexcavated, by a university research team conducting a survey of the area. He stabbed the wall of sandstone with a dagger, wondering how Operation Balghstaf had unraveled.

In the Middle East, Iran had yet to retaliate militarily for the destruction of Revolution Tower; rumors around Tehran of the destruction of London Bridge were the work of government propagandists. Talking heads on western television speculated that the attack may have strengthened moderates in the Iranian government and weakened the hard-liners. Polls in Great Britain indicated that the bombing was considered proportionate to the alleged Iranian government-sanctioned murder of Ambassador Lockhart. An exasperated Mortimer urged Prime Minister Lowe to mobilize the British navy in the Straits of Hormuz to inflame hostilities. He wanted Lowe to accuse Iran of mobilizing nuclear weapons and to, "declare war!"

In the western hemisphere, Balghstaf stalled when the Mexican government contained the emergency at the Puebla Nuclear Power Plant. They shut down the power plant, and invited an international team to assess safety and monitor radiation levels. A tour of the facility by President Delgado successfully calmed the populace. In the United States, the Baltimore train wreck slipped from the news cycle as the Carson administration adeptly batted away reports of a terrorist plot.

Mortimer stood in the hollow under the castle, and using the dagger etched out letters on the wall: K-A-S-H-M-I-R. He leaned against the wall, confident that Kashmir would revive Balghstaf and established a new standard for reaping.

Mortimer read *The Times* at Crumpets espresso bar in London over a bottle of Highland Spring Water, amused to sit among unsuspecting mortals. The ritual was important in devising the eastern component of Operation Balghstaf. A week-long special in the newspaper imparted an adequate understanding of the longstanding conflict between India and Pakistan over Kashmir. Straight away, Mortimer saw it as a "catalyst."

It amused him to learn that opposing claims on Kashmir were separated by a Line of Control. Lines and walls—Maginot Line, Belfast Peace Lines, Berlin Wall, Great Wall of Gorgon, Great Wall of China, Israel Security Wall—were easily manipulated instruments of death. When he visited the Himalayan Zone to conduct reconnaissance on Kashmir, Mortimer was astounded by its beauty, beguiled by the snow-peaked Himalayas and the lovely almond trees and cherry blossoms and the fields of saffron and meadows of wild flowers. Still, he had no qualms about plotting its destruction.

The completion of a hydroelectric dam by India in disputed territory threatened the primary source of irrigation for the fertile Punjab province of Pakistan. It represented an opportunity to Mortimer. The dam led to mass protests and outraged speeches, while Kashmirian separatists groups made plans to sabotage the structure. Mortimer monitored several groups, but the one that intrigued him most plotted a direct assault against India that might provoke a nuclear war.

A black Lincoln Town Car approached the Supreme Court of India. The driver showed proper identification to a policeman and parked in the VIP lot. Two terrorists from the Kashmir Liberation Brigade approached the building, unaware that Mortimer had already seized the souls of two security guards responsible for protecting the western hall.

At sixty four, Justice Altamas Rajput approached the age of mandatory retirement. He was a firm believer in the rights of the accused, and maintained a liberal perspective—an expert on classical Sanskrit literature, he frequently chaired the Sanskrit Talent Festival—and fit the ideal of a judge: urbane, cerebral, and a devoted family man.

Justice Dalveer Harsha, a stout man with an unruly beard, frequently criticized liberal policies as a detriment to Indian democracy. When appointed to the court, financial disclosure forms declared that he owned only a modest home. Somehow, on a government salary, he managed to accumulate vast amounts of valuable land, and as a result was regularly caricatured by the media as the face of corruption.

Following arguments on a case involving the right to privacy, Rajput and Harsha exited the court together, still wearing the traditional white neck bands and black silk coats. They maintained an awkward silence as they passed a gardener placing lotus flowers in a basin. As they turned a corner, the terrorists detonated the explosives within their briefcases and obliterated themselves, the gardener and both justices. The Supreme Court of India was scarred with a charred, smoldering hole—the indelible image went viral within the hour.

Following the attack, the Indian government issued statements of condemnation, and avowed its right to respond militarily against any state that may have sponsored the assault. Mortimer exulted when India mobilized army units along the Line of Control in Kashmir.

He spirited to Rashtrapati Bhavan, the residence of Prime Minister Raju. He listened attentively as the national security advisor reported that no group had yet claimed responsibility for the attack, but that it was highly probable that the attack was the work of a Kasmiri separatist group. Raju wanted to respond "aggressively, but prudently." When the national security advisor recommended a covert mission be organized, the defense minister angrily pointed out such a mission risked the lives of special operations personnel, whereas a ballistic missile aimed at Islamabad would kill terrorists and demonstrate to the world the consequences of attacking India.

Mortimer expected dark energy to convince the prime minister to bomb Pakistan. Standing next to a bust of Mahatmas Gandhi, however, Raju instead decided on a "limited" response. Mortimer wanted to reap the man, but dark energy forbade it, so he bitterly retreated to Nottingham Castle.

32

A trusted cohort of advisors provided General Aziz of Pakistan a wide variety of opinions over the crisis brought about by the assassination of two Indian Supreme Court justices. An ISI agent warned that India would exploit international condemnation of the attacks and use circumstantial evidence to blame Pakistan. One security advisor believed the incident would provide India an excuse to launch a wider attack in order to achieve its long-held ambition to establish control over all of Kashmir. General Aziz presented a calm facade, but he knew the situation was deteriorating rapidly. He requested solitude and time to pray.

Although the military-led government of Aziz had no involvement in the attack, the long history of hostilities and the wild celebration in the streets of Karachi after the bombing made it look as if Pakistan supported the terrorists—or sanctioned it. General Aziz declared martial law to tamp down the zeal of the populace.

During consultations, General Aziz had expressed confidence the superior training of the Pakistani soldiers would withstand any attack, but he understood the over-whelming tactical advantages of India. He moved around the office, admiring photographs of Lahore and the coast-line of Makran and smiled at a watercolor of Kashmir. It was strange how paradise stirred such trouble. He sat on a worn leather chair and caressed a bouquet of jasmine, wondering if he would ever experience peace.

Aziz pondered one unusual solution to the crisis: apol-ogize to India. Personally, he wanted to express regret for the cowardly assassinations, but he had sworn an oath to defend Pakistan. It already suffered from a severe drought and a deflated economy. Failure to manage the crisis had the potential to push the country down to the level of a failed state.

The general considered the consultations occurring in India. Prime Minister Raju would be advised that Pakistan had no capacity to win a military confrontation, and that it was led by a cultured man—Aziz was a graduate of Oxford, a wine connoisseur, a secularist, the patriarch of a prestigious family—who would act with reason. General Aziz decided he would use these suppositions as a tactical advantage and launch a preemptive nuclear strike against New Delhi.

33

Páll rarely received ordinary assignments. However, with 2nd and 3rd Tiers around the world at maximum capacity, he was called upon to complete several reapings.

He harvested Sáng, a twenty nine year-old immigrant from Vietnam, as he drove a tanker east to the Australian city of Adelaide on National Highway 94. Páll caused the man to have a stroke, and to please Mortimer, timed it so Sáng died as he drove around a turn in the road. The truck crashed down an embankment and exploded, releasing toxic smoke and inundating local hospitals with cases of respiratory failure.

The next assignment was nine hundred miles away on the east coast of Australia. As he spirited toward Sydney, Páll encountered a severe dust storm over the Tirari Desert. Swirling atmospheric pollutants included nitrogen dioxide, photochemical oxidants, carbon monoxide, and sulfur dioxide. The storm irreparably damaged the biographical scroll of the mortal, without it Páll had no address or detailed biography.

When he arrived in Sydney, he stole a suit hanging in an open apartment window and walked around the city, vexed that he would have to work to locate the assignment: Liam Flanagan.

34

Chief Ortega explored the ancient jails of London on foot, using a tourist guidebook. The walk eased his mind as he waited impatiently to rendezvous with Maximilian, and together proceed to Crumpets and arrest Mortimer. Ortega was disappointed by most of the sites though, such as Mashalsea Prison, which consisted of only a gate and one wall. Some had no structure whatsoever, only a marker to indicate its historical location.

Ortega felt he had collected enough circumstantial evidence to accuse Mortimer of unlawful activity, including but not limited to, unscheduled reapings, extended contact with a mortal and improper contact with an RD Team Member. It represented a tremendous opportunity. The arrest of a 1st Tier would prove the Policiá were essential to The Society of Death. It would raise the prestige of the department and prove it merited expansion. Privately, Ortega hoped he would be rewarded with a Vacation of a Lifetime and dreamed of living as a fisherman on the Canary Islands.

He was provided no protocol on arrests, but Ortega was unconcerned about due process, believing Grim Reapers operated on a higher plane than mortals. He expected Mortimer to cooperate; resistance would only exacerbate the situation. Nevertheless, Ortega came to London with an extra packet of salt.

The sound of church bells enchanted Ortega. He pondered the fate of his brother José, who died in England of typhoid while serving as an aide on a diplomatic mission. As he recalled, José was interred at St. Hyacinth Catholic Church and he wondered if the English government provided a headstone, possibly as a diplomatic gesture. Ortega skimmed the tourist guidebook and located St. Hyacinth in Pulmstead.

The church retained its distinctive tower made of ragstone, but windows that had held stained glass were bricked up, old doors once made of solid oak were shuttered with cheap plywood, and weeds smothered the land and covered over the headstones, most inscriptions were eroded. Ortega searched the churchyard, but found no evidence of a buried Spaniard. Undeterred, he decided to search the interior of the church. The nave was as neglected as the yard. Its tall wooden columns were damaged, and burial plaques were painted over with expletives. Prominent alcoves stood empty. Alerted by a dramatic drop in temperature, Ortega turned to face Roger Mortimer hovering over the disfigured pulpit.

"Evening, Chief Ortega." Mortimer held a new scythe made of dark violet-brown wood with veins of black and a subtle fragrance of roses. The blade was an elaborately carved piece of ivory. He held the scythe as if it were a scepter. "You've noticed my scythe."

It baffled Ortega how Mortimer anticipated the Policiá would be London.

"The wood of the handle comes from an endangered Brazilian tree," boasted Mortimer. "We must each do our part to destroy the environment." He came down from the pulpit and landed softly on the cracked marble floor. "I procured the blade from the Sa'dabad Palace of Iran. It was unguarded following the Event at Revolution Tower."

It was obvious by the smug reference to Iran that Mortimer had conspired to violate the Code of Conduct and The Book of Expiration Dates. The magnitude of the crime outraged Ortega. It went beyond the jurisdiction of the Policiá, but it was *he* who faced Mortimer. He considered removing a salt packet as a means of intimidation, but hesitated to provoke the 1st Tier.

"A long time ago St. Hyacinth was a beautiful church." Mortimer snickered. "Now look at it," he said, pointing to the warped parts of the ceiling and the broken angel wings over the altar.

"Sir, you know why I am in London," asserted Ortega. He no longer expected Mortimer to cooperate, and placed a hand over the pocket with the salt packets and prepared to strike.

"I respect your professional courtesy." Mortimer moved back a few steps. "When mortal, I was arrested with none of the professionalism you exhibit."

Ortega removed a salt packet.

"I assure you no salt will be necessary." As Mortimer carefully put down the exquisite scythe, Tristan material-ize and doused the Chief with saltwater from a plastic vial.

As parts of Ortega liquefied, laughter from Mortimer and Tristan echoed in the church. The left side of Ortega sizzled horrifically. He slithered around the floor and ran-dom droplets of saltwater opened a gap over his abdomen exposing the faux viscera. Ortega agonized, but he picked up the salt packet—a last duty, but was unable to open it. He thought of José. They would be together at St Hyacinth.

Mortimer moved toward Ortega. "You aligned with the wrong side Chief," he said. "I am the future of death."

What remained of Ortega slowed, came to a stop and turned to blue silt. Mortimer instructed Tristan to go to Trafalgar Square, and use the second vial to eliminate Maximilian, referring to the remainder of the Policiá as a "nuisance."

35

It was a hot morning. Already 79° Fahrenheit. Flanagan staggered out of a back room in the Prison Hulk Café after a weekend of socializing with ample amounts of Penfolds Grange at the Jewelry Emporium. He was hung-over, but promised Carolyn he would clean the fish tanks. He smiled when he saw Woggan.

"Hello Flanagan, I want to introduce the friends I told you about."

"Please invite them in."

Woggan waved to Cornelius and Kao, huddled together at the door.

"Um, g'day." Flanagan pointed to a table by a window with a pair of manacles and chains hanging over it, part of the ambiance of the Prison Hulk Café. Cornelius approached the table warily.

"You work with opals," Kao glanced at the jewelry display.

"Yes, young lady." Flanagan straightened out the placemats on the table. "I've worked with opals for over twenty years." He got up and returned holding a small pendant with purple, blue, and green tints that reminded Cornelius of an Egyptian ornament he saw on a painting at the workshop in Djoser. Flanagan handed it to Kao.

"Lovely." Kao caressed the opal.

"It has dazzling opalescence, a whole rainbow," noted Flanagan, accepting it back from Kao. He retrieved a set of small earrings and approached Kao. "Oh, your ears are not pierced," he said, glancing at her earlobes.

"No, I resisted all the trappings of traditional femininity."

Flanagan shrugged and lit a cigarette. He invited Cornelius to walk down a long hallway toward a small fish tank beyond the bar. "Look," said Flanagan, pointing to a plastic treasure chest with a tiny round opal. He picked it up. "Here," he said, handing it to Cornelius, "give it to the lady."

"Really?"

"Sure, even a ratbag like me can see you two are in love."

Cornelius massaged the opal. "Um, I have no way to pay," he said, embarrassed to accept such a luxury.

"You've had centuries to save, and you don't have one dollar?" Flanagan winked. "Anyway, don't worry, it's on me."

"I don't know what to say...thank you." Cornelius yearned to give it to Kao immediately but he put it in his pocket, saving it for a special occasion. They returned to the front of the café.

"Our time is limited," said Woggan. "My friends are…"

"Dead, right?" Flanagan laughed.

"I assure you, we are as alive as you." Kao lifted a small menu from between the salt and pepper shakers. "And hungry."

"Understood," said Flanagan with a nod.

Carolyn came to the table with a small menu. Kao ordered a biscuit with honey, porridge, and fried tomatoes. Cornelius ordered steak and eggs.

"Flanagan, my friends are in serious trouble," said Woggan.

"I know about trouble." Flanagan pulled up a sleeve and revealed a tattoo on his forearm of a dog resting atop a box. Cornelius anxiously checked his own forearms, grateful they were clear of any markings. He almost cried at the realization that he would never have an assignment again.

Kao peered at the image on Flanagan's arm. "It is a symbol."

"It's a jackal," he explained.

Cornelius saw a man capable of violence—it was both intimidating and reassuring.

"The symbol is Anubis," said Kao, "the Egyptian god responsible for protecting the dead on their journey to the afterlife." Cornelius vaguely recalled Páll talking about Anubis at the Cadet Workshop.

"I got it in prison as part of an initiation to a gang." Flanagan rolled down his sleeve. "Don't worry, it was only for breaking and entering."

"You broke something?" Cornelius asked.

"No, it means theft," said Kao, placing a hand on Cornelius; he realized he was prying.

"Enough 'bout me." Flanagan sat up straight. "So, you're in trouble?"

They were interrupted when Carolyn returned with a tray of food. Kao ate a biscuit with New Zealand black-currant jam on it, and Cornelius eagerly cut the streak. Woggan accepted a bottle of spring water, and Flanagan flipped through *The Sydney Morning Herald* on the table. A tall, skinny man peeked in the far window.

Flanagan left the table and walked over to the entrance. "Come in, we're open."

"Beautiful stones," remarked the man, looking at the display case.

"Opals." Flanagan accepted a mug from Carolyn, swallowed two aspirin and washed it down with espresso.

Carolyn turned to the man. "Would you like a menu, sir?"

"No, thank you." The man grinned awkwardly, revealing several broken teeth. "May I explore your shop?"

"Of course, please do." said Flanagan, yawning. He strolled across the café and sat back down at the table.

"My friends are outcasts among reapers," said Woggan. "They have no place to go."

"Sounds dangerous."

"Try to imagine an infuriated Grim Reaper," said Kao.

"I get it," said Flanagan, putting out the cigarette. "We'll have to get the two of you to a safe place"

Cornelius noticed Kao was staring down at her plate, covering her profile with the side of her hand, and almost spit out a piece of steak when he saw that the tall customer was Páll. They were caught.

"Flanagan!" Woggan jumped up and pointed. "Watch out! Grim Reaper!"

Páll moved toward Flanagan. "Prepare to die mortal."

"Not today, mate!" Flanagan reached into his tool-kit without looking, grabbed titanium calipers and hit the nearest fish tank, shattering the glass and releasing gallons of saltwater across the floor. Páll screamed and collapsed as his legs dissolved rapidly, causing him to fall backward onto the floor, and the saltwater to expose his vertebrae. He moaned, rolling left and right, unable to get away as if tangled in barbed wire, each movement intensified his suffering and exposed more viscera. Cornelius gagged, while Kao pulled what remained of Páll away from the saltwater, but it only postponed the inevitable.

Flanagan ran to the back of the café and told Carolyn to stay away and avoid the "incident." He returned and locked the front door, then collected the stranded fish and placed them in another tank.

Cornelius was stunned. "How did you...?"

"I remembered that Woggan feared saltwater," explained Flanagan. "The tank here was filled with the old brine."

"He came here for *you*?" Kao asked.

"Flanagan, my friend, you survived a Grim Reaper," said Woggan, moving to the rafters of the café, away from the saltwater.

"I guess I did," said Flanagan, proudly. "Imagine that?"

As far as Cornelius knew, there was no record of a human being ever destroying a Grim Reaper. Suddenly he realized a new danger existed. "The destruction of Páll will draw attention to the café," he said. "We have to get out of here!"

"I have a hut on an island off Tasmania," said Flanagan, "it's a real hideout." He checked the time. "We can be there for afternoon tea."

Kao examined the map on the wall of the café. "Is it Flinders Island?"

"You won't find it on that old map," said Flanagan. "It's *very* small, north of Tasmania in the Killiecrankie Bay. It's called Little Wallaby Island."

Cornelius joined Kao at the map.

"We can take a ferry from Melbourne to North Point on Flinders, then a boat to Little Wallaby Island," said Flanagan, opening a closet door and rummaging around the clutter. "The hut is small, but we'll make do." He pulled out a suitcase-sized box with compartments, and started packing the opals. "We'll do some prospecting," said Flanagan, packing a few hand-sized tools. "We can search for topaz crystals and quartz, and maybe find some surprises."

"I don't want any more surprises," said Cornelius.

Woggan came down from the rafters and stood next to Kao, careful to avoid a puddle of saltwater. "I will return to the escarpment."

"You are at risk, too," said Kao.

"My presence will increase your risk of capture."

"Woggan, please," begged Kao, "you have to come with us."

"Yeah, c'mon mate," said Flanagan. "I know how to hide."

"The three of you are now unrecorded in The Book of Expiration Dates, and have a real chance to survive," explained Woggan. "The longer I stay, the greater the danger."

There was silence.

Flanagan sighed heavily. "I'm glad to have known you," he said, wiping his nose.

"Me too, Opal Man."

"Thank you for everything you did for us," said Cornelius.

A tearful Kao hugged Woggan.

"Goodbye my friends." Woggan smiled weakly, and stepped out of the café.

Kao swept up the granular remains of Páll and mixed it with the gravel at the bottom of the broken fish tank. Flanagan explained to Carolyn over shots of whiskey what had happened, and why he had to flee to Little Wallaby Island. Cornelius watched Sky News on a TV in the kitchen as it reported on a crisis between India and Pakistan. It was strange. He saw no tell-tale signs, but he felt the crisis was orchestrated by a Grim Reaper. As Kao cleaned up the glass shards, and Flanagan organized their escape to Little Wallaby Island, Cornelius read blurbs in the International News section of the newspaper about the events—*the Events*—of the last week. He put the paper down, convinced it all added up to a plot by Roger Mortimer, as Houdon had predicted.

Cornelius yearned to live with Kao, but the knowledge that millions of lives were at risk made it impossible to simply move to Little Wallaby Island. It was insane, that he, a farmer from colonial Massachusetts, a bungling Grim Reaper Cadet, and now a man with no skills relevant to the modern world, would even try to stop a catastrophe engineered by a satanic Grim Reaper.

36

Standing at the corner of Spring Street and the Avenue of the Americas in Greenwich Village, New York, wearing a pinstriped suit, Mortimer eagerly watched the news on a plasma TV in a window of an electronics store. He stood outside the store surrounded by mortals—one extremely muscled man might one day serve as a palace guard, one voluptuous woman might serve as a concubine, another, a matronly woman, as a laundress, and an elderly man, a gardener. When he departed India, Mortimer had lost hope of an Indo-Pakistani war, but dark energy had somehow manipulated the situation and caused Pakistan to attack with a nuclear weapon. It was a dark miracle.

Mortimer purposefully chose to wait for the outcome of the attack in the Zone of Manhattan. He originally established it as the Zone of New Amsterdam; reaperkind ignored previous inconsequential explorations of the western hemisphere. As a young reaper, he had accompanied Captain Hudson on the *Half Moon* to the southern tip of Manhattan in 1609 with instructions to reap several frontier hunters. It was part of an agreement with The Great

Spirit of the Beaver to shield the rodents from merciless exploitation by the Dutch, who hunted the creature to produce waterproof hats from its fur and medicine from its anal secretions.

The colony prospered and provided limitless opportunities for an ambitious Grim Reaper. Over the centuries, as areas of responsibility in North America were drawn and redrawn, and assignments shifted, Mortimer held tight to Manhattan, overjoyed by the capricious leveling of hills, draining of wetlands, and stripping away of trees, all to lay down a suffocating blanket of asphalt. At twenty three square miles, the area of responsibility was among the smallest in the world (officially a microzone), but it was rich with the souls of entertainers, authors, philanthropists, athletes, politicians and diplomats.

Mortimer plied Manhattan Island from 1609 to 1775, when, at the beginning of the American Revolution, he received an Allowance to Act Mortal. He planned to go to Versailles and observe the opulence of King Louis XVI, but he decided to stay, lured by the rebellion of the colonists. It was a hot July 9th, 1776 in Lower Manhattan when he witnessed a public reading of the odious Declaration of Independence. Mortimer had no sympathy for George III but he was offended as an Englishman when, whipped up by the hypocritical rhetoric, a mob of mortals toppled a statue of the king wearing a Roman toga. Mortimer exacted a measure of revenge on a humid August day, helping General Howe defeat the colonials in the Battle of Long Island by posing as a farmer and relaying knowledge of an unguarded pass.

In 1863, Mortimer enjoyed another Allowance to Act Mortal in the city by inciting the draft riots. On the second day of drawing draft numbers to enlist men in the Union army, a drunken mob protested at the office of the Provost Marshall on 3rd Avenue and 47th Street, and although repulsed by the Irish, Mortimer posed as a firefighter of the Black Joke Engine Company 33. He heaved a huge paving stone at the window of the draft office and helped the crowd set the building ablaze, next he climbed telegraph poles—swiftly, without risk of injury—to cut the lines and prevent the transmission of warnings to the rest of the city.

Mortimer made plans to reap the secretary-general of the United Nations when he called for an Emergency Special Session to calm the situation and requested nations deliver radiation treatment kits to India. However, Mortimer was encouraged when President Carson made a statement on television substantiating reports of a nuclear "incident" over the Indian city of Bhiwani.

He was overjoyed by news from around the world: authoritarian regimes used the crisis as an excuse to impose martial law and harass opposition groups, Europe shut its stock markets over rumors of impending terrorist attacks, and air travel in the United States came to a halt because of anonymous calls stating that a "dirty bomb" was planted on an unspecified commercial airliner. Chaos reigned.

Mortimer walked up Lafayette Street to Union Square and sat at a restaurant in the Flatiron District, ordered a Pinot Noir of deep crimson and enjoyed its delicate scent of dark fruits and spices, daydreaming of hundreds of millions of deaths. He had always wanted to transform Systematic Multiple Reapings to Systematic *Mass* Reapings, and hoped to include China and Russia, and ultimately the United States, in the coming Indo-Pakistani war. The crisis would require time to reach its apex, so Mortimer decided to indulge a tour of Manhattan.

He left the petite waitress, a bed-warmer in the coming kingdom, a $100 bill and walked up Broadway, and resisted the urge to spirit over the bedlam of Herald Square with its pedestrians and taxis, trucks and bicyclists.

He stopped at the Museum of Natural History. Although it was hard to comprehend an age without reapers and mortals, fossilized remains of saber tooth tigers, mastodons, and dinosaurs made it incontrovertible. He drank Universal Elixir from a water fountain, and speculated on the possibility of restoring the southern tip of Manhattan to conditions of the 18th century, perhaps as a project for a talented mortal.

When details of the nuclear blast over India emerged Mortimer was apoplectic.

The radiation around Bhiwani was severe. Eighteen hundred people in the city were killed within a half-mile radius of the spot where the warhead landed, and an unpredictable number were destined to suffer and die slowly. According to the Pentagon and State Department of the United States, it would have been much worse if the warhead had not malfunctioned. It exploded high enough in the atmosphere to limit the impact, preventing hundreds of thousands of additional causalities.

Meanwhile, Pakistan initially issued a statement of denial, but it changed course and expressed regret, accompanied by an explanation of how a rogue general had ordered the attack. The confession created enough reason for India to delay an immediate and overwhelming military response.

Mortimer spirited to Pennsylvania Station, and down the escalators to a train tunnel. Filled with rage, he screamed almost as loud as an arriving Amtrak train. The station was crowded with Columbus Day shoppers and the usual rush-hour commuters. He wanted to derail a train and kill hundreds, but instead shoved just one mortal down onto the tracks of the 5:33 train to Far Rockaway. He compartmentalized the rage and headed to Washington D. C., wondering what had happened to Páll.

Mortimer had anticipated the possibility that America would intervene to limit hostile action by India or Pakistan, and sent Páll to monitor the U.S. navy. If necessary, Páll was to seize the soul of Vice Admiral Woodcock of the Fifth Fleet on the USS Truman. If he had done so, it would have delayed the American naval response—shooting down the nuclear warhead—long enough to allow it to explode at the optimal trajectory over New Delhi.

Mortimer arrived in Washington to eavesdrop on President Carson, anxious to salvage Balghstaf. He moved around the Oval Office, ignoring President Carson at work editing a speech, and noticed a miniature of the famous painting *Declaration of Independence* by John Trumbull. If he were in command of British forces during the revolution, he would have had George Washington assassinated.

When CIA Director Thompson arrived, Mortimer moved to the desk of the president. Carson congratulated Thompson on the use of a spy satellite to gain the intelligence that allowed the USS Truman to shoot down the Pakistani warhead. Mortimer seethed as the president updated Thompson on the extraordinary attitude of Prime Minister Ragu—despite the assassination of the judges, and the nuclear missile—India still had a desire to act against Pakistan with a measured response, one so limited it would demonstrate to the Pakistani people that India wanted to use the recent incident as "an excuse to launch peace."

"Remarkable, Madame President," said Thompson. "What can we do at the CIA to help?"

"I have an idea," said President Carson, "but there's a catch."

"What?"

"It will involve a Republican."

"Oh crap," said Thompson, laughing.

President Carson smiled, and pressed the intercom to her secretary. "Timothy?"

"Yes, Madame President."

"Please call Ben Rosenthal," said President Carson. "It's urgent."

Mortimer detested President Carson. How dare a woman impede Operation Balghstaf.

Rosenthal was the representative of the 4th district of Oklahoma, and a veteran of Iraq and Afghanistan. He was a retired Major League Baseball pitcher who lost two prime years when he joined the National Guard. As an avid hunter and a member of the NRA, Ben Rosenthal made headlines when he sponsored a bill to buy back fire-arms, and possessed the rarest of traits among American politicians: gravitas. Most significantly, he and Prime Minister Raju were old friends from the London School of Economics, and President Carson and Thompson agreed, the ideal choice to act as a special envoy to India.

When Rosenthal arrived at the White House, President Carson inquired about a bill on farming subsidies, but the representative from Oklahoma waved away the words.

"Pardon, Madam President, with all due respect to farming, you and I both know I am here because of my friendship with Prime Minister Raju. How may I serve my country?"

Following an update by CIA Director Thompson, the president asked Rosenthal to "hand-deliver" intelligence illegally obtained by the CIA to the Indian prime minister, "to avert a war on the subcontinent."

Rosenthal accepted the task, and as he left the White House, Mortimer ached to stop the transmission of intelligence by killing the Oklahoman. Mortimer pleaded with dark energy, and suggested methods to make it appear authentic, but the request was ignored. The cold rebuke alarmed Mortimer.

37

Recalling that generations of relatives fished off the Sanriku Coast of Japan, Kao was ashamed to vomit on the ferry ride to Flinders Island. Flanagan was as tender as a father, guiding her to the side rail away from the exhaust of the engines, and getting a few crackers to settle her stomach.

"Welcome to Flinders," he said, disembarking from the ferry. Flanagan carried an oversized backpack and a First Aid Kit.

"I thought we were heading to Little Wallaby Island?" Kao was relieved to set foot on land, and dreaded the prospect of another ferry ride.

"We will daughter, but have to get provisions here in Whitemark."

It was awkward to travel to an isolated region with a virtual stranger, but Kao felt reassured by the word "daughter." Flanagan pointed to a ramshackle store at the edge of a picturesque street. He bought an apple and handed it to Kao, and proceeded to buy four bags of groceries, including several packs of spices, "to cook fish."

They walked over to a boat launch and paid a man for the short ride—mercifully short as far as Kao was concerned—to Little Wallaby. As it came into view, the island reminded Kao of peaceful summers on the island of Nii-jima playing with cousins and building sandcastles. Flanagan pointed to a path. Kao enjoyed the abundance of butterflies along the way.

They arrived at the small hut. Kao found it charming, certainly a home compared to the steel cabin on Kamchatka. It was approximately five hundred square feet, and had a loft with a bed and a lovely armoire with a carving of Mount Killiekrankie. Flanagan claimed the less inviting futon on the main level and insisted that Kao take the upstairs. The hut was clean and equipped with a kitchenette and a propane-fueled generator for heat and hot water, but no bathroom, only an outhouse. A plastic tub held a few small shovels and sieves to collect "Killiekrankie diamonds" on the beach, and a circle of stones formed a fire pit. Simple and elegant.

"It so close to the water, Cornelius will love it," said Kao, imaging them swimming together.

"I bet he will," said Flanagan. "Do you like it?"

"It is a lovely home." Kao wanted time alone with Cornelius when he returned and hoped Flanagan would go to Flinders Island on occasion, maybe for provisions or to visit the local pub. "You are so kind to help us."

Flanagan smiled. "Um, we've got a boat," he said, pointing to a blue kayak in the scrub next to a dry stream-bed. "I'm going to unpack and catch our supper. Why don't you explore the island before it gets dark? Tomorrow morning we have to go to Whitemark to get more fuel."

"Okay, I will."

"Everything will be all right, you'll see."

"Thank you." Kao kicked off her sneakers and walked to the shoreline barefoot. The water was cold.

The island was beautiful. The wet sand underfoot was soothing. Kao climbed over several boulders to a secluded spot and sat. It was a good place to meditate, but it was impossible—her mind replayed over and over the stiff farewell with Cornelius at Sydney Airport, and the empty feeling of wanting to hug, but feeling too embarrassed at the crowded ticket counter.

The sun eased below the horizon, and a crescent moon emerged from a cloud. It gave Kao a frightening vision of a scythe hanging over the world. "No, I refuse to believe it."

An area of sand rippled by the wind and bordered by two rivulets led to a rush of inspiration. Kao collected seashells, and down on her hands and knees, pushed up piles of sand and filled the circle with bright rocks, adding the shells to produce the image of a radiant sun.

"Oh please Cornelius," she said, looking up at the stars, "come back to me."

38

Qantas Airways Flight 29 from Sydney to London experienced routine turbulence, but Cornelius was terrified and kept the seatbelt fastened throughout the flight. Spiriting was easy; flying in a tin can was torturous. He regretted the trip. It was stupid to suppose he would be able to put a stop to the monstrous Mortimer. Cornelius had decided to go to Great Britain based on nothing on little more than the memory of Mortimer yelling at Ayodele during a movie about the depiction of Nottingham Castle. Cornelius kicked the seat in front of him, causing the occupant, a priest, to turn around. Cornelius held an old Natick prejudice against "papists", but he was embarrassed and apologized to the man.

It was a long flight. He tried to sleep, but it was impossible. At the transfer in Dubai he bought a box of duty-free dominoes and for the remainder of the flight read the instructions on the complicated games he had always avoided playing at the Replanting Department.

Cornelius wandered around Heathrow Airport. He bought a ticket for the National Express Bus to Nottingham, and reluctantly climbed aboard. He took a window seat and slumped down. The last trip on a bus led to Delaware and the Excruciating Death of Dr. ZZ. He felt crippled by guilt, haunted by images of the man suffering. Now, as he rode another bus, Cornelius became fully conscious of why he had decided to try and stop Mortimer. He had to atone.

It was quiet at Nottingham Castle. Cornelius He longed to be with Kao. He rambled about the grounds, unshaven and unwashed. There was no castle, only a mansion with a few tourists. He wanted to give up when he saw the list of upcoming activities at Nottingham: weddings, art shows, staged medieval jousts, concerts—hardly the home of a Grim Reaper. He had traveled half-way round the world on the slim chance Mortimer would be at the old castle. Foolish. He tossed the small box of dominoes in a trash bin. Helpless, he lay face down on the soft lawn, comforted by the smell of grass and dirt.

39

While Ben Rosenthal relayed the critical intelligence to Prime Minster Raju, an Indian Sukhoi Su-30MKI fighter flew within range of the Pakistani capital, awaiting orders. Five additional fighters flew over Lahore, Karachi, Peshawar, Faisalabad, and Rawalpindi. The conversation between the old friends occurred over a cup of tea. Mortimer eavesdropped as Rosenthal, acting as a special envoy of the President Carson, told Raju that a grateful United States would reward the demonstration of restraint by India with advanced technologies to upgrade the Indian Air Force. The old friends chatted about their days at the London School of Economics, and Rosenthal revealed to Raju the *exact* location of General Aziz in real time. When the Indian PM nodded, Mortimer understood that Indian retaliation would consist of a targeted assassination of the Pakistani general. Dejected, Mortimer exited out a window, exasperated by the complexities of modern-day international diplomacy.

The targeted killing of General Aziz by Indian commandos virtually put a stop to Operation Balghstaf. India was avenged, and though Pakistan expressed outrage at the "invasion" and activated army troops east of Lahore, it refrained from mobilizing its air defenses. Around the world, the retaliation was praised for protecting the lives of millions of civilians; within India, reaction was mixed, and included violent unrest and one failed assassination attempt against Prime Minister Raju.

The end of Operation Balghstaf devastated Mortimer.

A war between India and Pakistan was to be the foundation of the new age. It held the potential to create a worldwide conflict. He felt abandoned by dark energy.

Moving up to the clouds, Mortimer considered one last move. It was crude, but it would achieve an immediate reduction of the mortal population and possibly reignite the passion of dark energy. He spirited west towards Great Britain.

It was almost dawn over Zaporizhia, Ukraine. Mortimer approximated that the city was half the distance from India to London, and went down to the banks of the Dnieper River to refuel with Universal Elixir, long overdue, he was dehydrated and almost collided with a 737. Sunrise was seconds away. For a moment, Mortimer lamented the voracious desire he had to rule, but as if by some incontrovertible law of physics, self-pity was replaced by scheming to achieve the status of king. He jumped to the clouds, unconcerned by the gaze of a small boy milking a cow.

The mysterious disappearance of Páll gnawed at Mortimer, and as he passed Germany he changed course and headed to the Svalbard archipelago. Arriving at the Dwelling, he was perplexed by its condition. It had thawed and chambers were barely recognizable. Though haggard, Mortimer straightened up and stood regally. "Cadet Tristan!" he bellowed.

"Yes sir?" Tristan emerged chewing ice and dragging the scythe with the blade pointed down, scratching it across the rough terrain. Such impudence merited a severe reprimand, but Mortimer needed the services of the potent cadet.

"I wanted to inquire as to the outcome of your encounter with the reaper of the Policiá."

"I got 'em both."

"Excellent." Mortimer ignored the insouciance and circled around Tristan. "I have another important assignment: You will visit Australia and..." Mortimer slipped and almost fell. "Pardon, I...I am dehydrated." He leaned down and picked up a chip of ice. "Tristan, your next assignment will be to expel Woggan the Observer. He may be responsible for the death of our esteemed colleague Páll."

"What happened?"

"I have no specific intelligence," responded Mortimer, exasperated. "Your instructions are to destroy the Observer. You will find him near his ancestral home on the east coast of Australia."

"Okay, got it." Tristan moved a step, but stopped and turned. "What about Cornelius?"

"We have no time to search for the insubordinate cadet," said Mortimer, detecting a way to motivate the cadet. "After you complete the assignment regarding Woggan, I grant you the right to conduct the Expulsion of the Cornelius Hoyt."

Tristan smiled wickedly.

Mortimer drifted high over Great Britain, noticing the lights of the cities burned maize-yellow, as if lit by a trillion candles; he thought it was strange that mortals were afraid of the dark. When he landed in London, he saw that newspaper headlines on the resolution of the Pakistan-India crisis and news of the ouster of the hard-line president in Tehran. He rushed to 10 Downing Street.

40

Prime Minster Lowe suffered heart palpitations following the meeting with Mortimer. The Grim Reaper was deranged. Lowe wanted no part of redeploying a Vanguard class submarine with sixteen trident missiles to the harbor in Dhekelia, a British-administered base on Cyprus—Mortimer would hijack the sub or cause it to fire a missile. Lowe trembled with horror at the possible targets: Istanbul or Ankara, Cairo or Jerusalem. Moscow? Beijing? Washington D.C.? London! Lowe temporarily appeased Mortimer when he placed a call to the secretary of state for defense to make arrangements for an "urgent meeting" about the Middle East. He assured Mortimer redeployment of a nuclear submarine was possible, but explained he was legally required to consult with his cabinet first.

Lowe caressed a bust of Winston Churchill. "What am I to do?" he asked the sculpture. He lit a cigar, poured a brandy and imagined the great statesman commanding: Resolve to be resolute! Lowe proudly put on a Union Jack lapel pin. The situation was unacceptable. He would refuse

Mortimer and redeploy the submarine out of range of the Middle East, and extend some kind of olive branch to the new Iranian president.

Enough was enough. To hell with Mortimer.

41

Cornelius slept unnoticed for two hours on the lawn of Nottingham Castle. Jetlagged, he attempted to go back to sleep, but he was cold and starving. He walked around, a solitary tourist without a camera or cell phone, avoiding the bright faux gas lights placed around the mansion. He read a sign about caves under the castle and turned to walk the opposite way—he had had enough of caves. He walked leisurely past a Victorian grandstand and imagined holding hands with Kao and listening to music.

He noticed a white line stretching down the manicured lawn, and wondering if it led to an exit, followed it, but it stopped at an overgrown rhododendron. Cornelius touched the line. It was cold! He turned to run, but the ground gave way and he fell in a hole, up to his waist. He tried to scramble up but slid straight down, spitting out dirt as he plummeted down to hard ground. Cornelius rubbed the dirt out of his eyes and became aware of the subzero temperature—Mortimer!

The revitalized body that felt wonderful in Australia now felt as though it would explode. Heart and lungs

pulsated with a heavy beat. Cornelius shivered uncontrollably. He had a fleeting vision of riding Arabella bareback.
It was unreal. He was dead again.

He recovered enough to attempt an escape by pulling on a tangle of roots, but they were short and stringy.
Petrified, he wanted to pray, but he had no words. He was
buried alive.

42

The dank cave under Nottingham was a constant reminder to Mortimer that he lived as a peasant while he awaited the coming kingdom. When it came, he would have a luxurious palace, and as promised by dark energy, be rewarded with the capacity to indulge mortal appetites. He lit a torch and gazed at the rudimentary map of the world he had etched on a wall. He made clever use of several cracks in the stone: one approximated the east coast of North America, one the west coast of Africa. England was at the center. The crude map served a vital purpose.

Mortimer turned when he heard sound coming from a remote part of the cave. He carefully placed the scythe made of ivory and rosewood against the wall, and picked up a sword.

As king, Mortimer decided he would replace the dull scythe—the tool of serfs—with the regal sword. As the original instrument of European Grim Reapers, ancient swords still possessed the power to destroy a reaper. Mortimer acquired a pair from an ill-fated treasure hunter. He picked up the longer of the two swords, and slashed at an imaginary adversary.

43

Tristan spirited to Australia, unshackled by Tracking, eager to exploit the chance to get away from the cadet program. Mortimer disabled the tracking signal on Tristan to enable him to hunt Woggan without the risk of surveillance.

As acolytes of Mortimer, Tristan and Russell agreed to work together whenever practical to survive the tempestuous 1st Tier. It was Russell who told Tristan that Páll went missing on an assignment to reap Liam Flanagan in Australia. It explained the assignment to expel Woggan—he must have helped the mortal. Regardless, Tristan had a private agenda.

Tristan was recruited on a rainy night in 1968. He and his parents and younger brother Tomi had vacationed in Italy and were heading home from the Ontario International Airport. He was in the backseat of the Oldsmobile with Tomi when a truck hauling fuel hit them. Their car flipped over a guardrail on Highway 101 and Tristan burned slowly—an Excruciating Death. The daily Residual Images of the crash, including the screams of Tomi and his parents, were torturous. It made Tristan want to kill. And kill and kill. While Mortimer bargained with dark energy to rule the world, Tristan wanted only to ruin it.

Tristan learned only recently from Páll that he was recruited as a result of pocketing a domino. As an artifact of reaperkind, it was considered a risk to the integrity of the Wall. When Tristan was told the domino came from Cornelius, he wanted immediate retribution—but it was impossible without incurring Expulsion. It was hard to wait, but he regularly imagined slow, torturous ways of killing Cornelius. The time had finally come.

Tristan went to the Sydney Opera House and rested atop its strange roof, struck by how the structures resembled the tips of scythes. He rechecked the scroll that Russell had stolen from the RD. Tristan determined that if he located Liam Flanagan he would find Woggan—after all, the mortal must have had help to survive a reaping. He located the Prison Hulk Café and searched for Liam Flanagan without success. Frustrated, Tristan crumpled the scroll. He had one last place to search for Woggan, and spirited to the home the mortal kept on a tiny islet off Tasmania.

44

Mortimer recognized the uniquely high-pitched sound Ayodele made when materializing.

"Welcome, Master." Mortimer stood holding the sword.

"What are we to do with you, Roger?" Ayodele placed both hands within the wide sleeves of the cloak, the blasé posture irritated Mortimer. "You have changed," claimed Ayodele.

"No." Gradually, Mortimer raised the sword. It glistened in the glow of the torch. He calculated the reach of the Master, aware his arms were long enough to strike from a distance. "I have always wanted power."

"Oh, I understand, Roger. By change, I mean... mutated." Ayodele glanced at the sword resting against the wall. "You do understand that you were poisoned by the contaminated water of the Dnieper River in the Ukraine?" The remark flustered Mortimer. He listened as Ayodele explained how the Soviet Union had used the river as a source of hydroelectric power in the production of steel and aluminum, and as a result it contained high levels of toxins. "As you know Roger, our ranks are depleted, but you have failed to appreciate accidental poisonings are one of the factors." Ayodele glowered. "It seems fitting that your contemptuous attitude towards nature now plagues you."

Mortimer smiled—aware it would aggravate Ayodele—and to show he understood the claims about poison were a ploy to gain an advantage. "I wanted to change, Master, or mutate as you say. I will be a hybrid of mortal and reaper. And you, Master? You will make your contribution to dusk." Mortimer moved to an open area of the cave.

"A fair fight?" Ayodele picked up the second sword. "How chivalrous of you, I had no idea you were capable of acting with honor."

"The future of death has come," proclaimed Mortimer, churning with rage, "and you will have no place to exist!"

"Perhaps, Roger, but I believe the future rests with the Provocateurs." Ayodele raised the sword and pointed it at Mortimer.

Splendid, thought Mortimer. If Ayodele were the long-rumored 1st Tier aligned with the Provocateurs, he would sunder the resistance movement by killing its leader. He slashed at the Master. The loud strike of swords created enough vibration to cause several rocks to crash down.

As they parried, Mortimer maneuvered Ayodele so he was positioned against the wall containing the etching of the world map.

45

A deafening clash of swords.

Against instinct, Cornelius crawled toward the light, both hands and knees bled on the rough ground—an ordinary pain compared to the absolute terror he felt as he approached the duel.

46

Ayodele leaned against the map on the wall.

"Now!" yelled Mortimer.

Russell spirited out of a crack with an unsealed tube of salt and struck Ayodele in the back.

Mortimer moved away, sword down, transfixed by the tableau. Ayodele fell to his knees, dropped the sword and grabbed at the hole created by the salt as if to staunch blood loss. Mortimer wanted to savor the spectacle of a fragmented Master, but centuries of waiting made it impossible. He raised the sword high and slashing wildly, cut off the head of Ayodele. The legendary Grim Reaper of sixteen centuries turned to a fine platinum dust.

"Sire, we have succeeded!" exclaimed Russell, raising both arms high.

Mortimer always appreciated an easy target, and swung the sword and halved the cadet. Russell crumpled as easy as an empty cardboard box. Mortimer strutted around the cave. "I will have a throne to rival a pharaoh…a palace beyond the beauty of the Taj Mahal…I will be feted with epic feasts and orgies to exceed a sultan!"

Mortimer tore off the cloak, revealing the emerald and gold tunic of the brigade he led when he conquered England. He stood regally and held the sword up straight as if posing for a portrait.

47

Linnaeus stayed silent, hidden in a crevice of the cave, distraught over the murders of Ayodele and Russell. He had tracked Russell to Nottingham utilizing a "tag" devised from elements in the RD, based on the suspicion that he was associating with the Traditionalists and committing a flagrant violation of the mission of the Replanting Department. He was sickened to learn of the extent that Russell had conspired with Mortimer. Were they responsible for the deaths of Hale and Sebastian?

As he attempted to sort out the momentous developments, Linnaeus watched Mortimer dart around the cave swinging the sword, strangely charged, as if an unstable element. He hypothesized the 1st Tier had contracted a malady with no suitable classification.

Linnaeus was stunned when Cornelius emerged from the dark, almost unrecognizable with a rough beard.

Mortimer pointed his sword at Cornelius. "I will slay you!"

Linnaeus spirited out of the fissure and intentionally knocked a torch off the wall, causing Mortimer to turn around.

48

Cornelius instinctively reached down and picked up the sword of Ayodele and lunged, striking Mortimer in the center of his chest.

"You bastard!" screamed Mortimer. He clutched at the sword and pulled it out. A putrid grey fluid poured out of the gash.

Cornelius moved away. Mortimer fragmented to a lump of skin and bones, but his eyes were still vibrant. Though terrified, Cornelius picked up the sword. He leaned over Mortimer, drew the blade across his own index finger and bled. "You were killed by a mortal!"

Mortimer had no capacity to respond, but the eyes widened with recognition. It lasted but a moment, and then he turned into a pile of dirt.

Traumatized, Cornelius walked over to what remained of Ayodele, knelt, and gathered up the soft, rust-colored dust. Unsteady, he crawled to the hole leading out of the cave and rolled a few rocks over to use as steps. He climbed up and out onto the lawn of Nottingham Castle.

The plastic card Flanagan had provided still contained inexplicable value. It permitted Cornelius to pay the bus fare to the airport, and when he arrived at Heathrow, to buy an airline ticket to Australia and a plate of fish and chips.

It was a long journey. Though barely conscious during the trip, again and again, whenever he awakened, he double-checked every pocket, saddened that he lost the opal from Flanagan. He had wanted to give it to Kao when he got to Little Wallaby Island.

49

As instructed by the Triumvirate, 1st Tiers around the world disseminated an "official" account of the recent extraordinary developments:

Ayodele expelled a treasonous Mortimer, guilty of a vast conspiracy against The Society of Death. It was the last momentous achievement of the Master, as he subsequently reached Termination while spiriting over Africa.

Carl Linnaeus was promoted to 1st Tier in recognition of destroying the co-conspirator Páll.

Cadets Cornelius Hoyt and Kao were killed while destroying the duplicitous Tristan and Russell.

The Triumvirate mandated that Linnaeus keep secret the truth about the incident at the castle, and the fact that the rogue cadet Tristan still existed. Most of all, Linnaeus swore to keep secret the unfathomable transformation of Cornelius and Kao back into mortals.

For his service, Linnaeus was promoted and awarded a Vacation of a Lifetime. He selected to live as an amateur naturalist in Australia. He always wanted to explore the flora and fauna of the "Great Southern Land" and planned on attending a symposium of the International Commission of Zoological Nomenclature. Most importantly, he selected Australia to protect a grieving Cornelius.

Linnaeus speculated it was Tristan who caused the explosion on the small boat that killed both Liam Flanagan and Kao. The motive was unclear, but he deduced that Tristan may have intended to kill Cornelius, and only accidentally came upon the pair while they were crossing Bass Straight to Little Wallaby Island.

Theoretically, as an unrecorded mortal in The Book of Expiration Dates, Cornelius existed beyond the bounds of The Society of Death, but Linnaeus decided to operate under the assumption that Tristan still posed a threat.

Linnaeus completed two last placements before he left the RD. He transmuted the soul of Liam Flanagan to a strutting peacock at a bird sanctuary in New Zealand. Kao was a unique case—the only mortal to twice experience the touch of a Grim Reaper. It gratified Linnaeus when he successfully transmuted the luminous soul of Kao to a life as a dolphin. He only wished he was permitted to tell Cornelius.

50

As Woggan spirited over the escarpment, the whole of the reaper body he had inhabited for 1,697 years evaporated, particle by particle, until he was part of the sky.

He was conscious of family and friends and flowers. Of hurling a boomerang on a lazy day under the sun. Of singing and dancing by the fire. Simple love. Dreamtime.

51

Cornelius found a chisel stored in a box on the porch, and sat on a step and carved the walrus tusk. Little Wallaby Island was a tranquil refuge. Filled with fish, wild berries, and freshwater. The cottage had a small garden with peppers and cucumbers. The island had everything. And nothing.

The sun sank below the horizon, and the sky turned dark violet blue. A warm breeze and a chorus of cicadas kept Cornelius at work on the tusk. He was tired. When it resembled Arabella he placed it on the shelf over the bed.

It was late. Alive and alone, he lay down and wept.

www.ingramcontent.com/pod-product-compliance
Lightning Source LLC
Chambersburg PA
CBHW032210190626
46810CB00019B/2429